MOBBED UP 3

Lock Down Publications and Ca$h Presents

Mobbed Up 3

A Novel by *King Rio*

Lock Down Publications

P.O. Box 944
Stockbridge, Ga 30281
www.lockdownpublications.com

Lock Down Publications
Like our page on Facebook: Lock Down Publications @
www.facebook.com/lockdownpublications.ldp
Book interior design by: **Shawn Walker**
Edited by: **Jill Alicea**

Stay Connected with Us!

Text **LOCKDOWN** to 22828 to stay up-to-date with new releases, sneak peaks, contests and more…
Thank you!

Submission Guideline.

Submit the first three chapters of your completed manuscript to ldpsubmissions@gmail.com, subject line: Your book's title. The manuscript must be in a .doc file and sent as an attachment. Document should be in Times New Roman, double spaced and in size 12 font. Also, provide your synopsis and full contact information. If sending multiple submissions, they must each be in a separate email.

Have a story but no way to send it electronically? You can still submit to LDP/Ca$h Presents. Send in the first three chapters, written or typed, of your completed manuscript to:

LDP: Submissions Dept
P.O. Box 944
Stockbridge, Ga 30281

DO NOT send original manuscript. Must be a duplicate.

Provide your synopsis and a cover letter containing your full contact information.

Thanks for considering LDP and Ca$h Presents.

Prologue
January 3rd 2016
Sunday 10:17 A.M.

There were just over fifty people attending the burial of David and Susan Owens at Rosehill Cemetery.

This day, the weather was no different from the other days of this Windy City winter. A four-inch layer of snow covered the ground like a thick cake frosting, and the temperature had it feeling like the very opposite of hell.

Rell sat in the front row between his girlfriend, Tamera Lyon, and his mother, dressed in a dapper black suit and smelling like the ounce of Kush he and Jah had smoked before driving here. The dark Louis Vuitton sunglasses he had on were meant to hide his tears, but they still rolled down his handsome brown face. Jah was also crying. Both of them had loved their father unconditionally. Just before his death, he'd bought them a house, and he'd given Rell the matte black Escalade that they had arrived in here to the burial.

In death, David "Big Man" Owens and his wife Susan had left Rell and Jah a lot more.

The couple had expired just over a week ago in a car accident during a Miami vacation. Rell had gotten the news early that morning, at a time when he himself had been going through so much drama in the streets of Chicago that he wasn't sure if he'd make it to see the next day.

The dreadful call came from a Miami police detective who'd suspected that Susan might have been drugged and possibly raped shortly before the crash, and it turned out he was right. The autopsy revealed a massive dose of Thorazine in Susan's blood, along with the DNA of a serial rapist who'd traveled to Miami from California and was still on the loose.

The preacher from the church Rell and Jah had attended growing up was quoting a passage from the Holy Bible. Maria, their mother, was sobbing miserably, though she and their father had not been on good terms for years. Rell put an arm around her shoulders and pulled her close.

"It's gon' be okay, Momma," he murmured gently, rocking forth and back, rubbing a hand up and down from her shoulder to her elbow.

Tamera's smartphone rang, interrupting the service, and she quickly shut off the ringer and apologized. Rell gave her the side-eye, but kept quiet.

Jah could not take it. He got up halfway through the service, and with a tear-streaked face, he went and climbed in the backseat of the SUV. Tirzah, Rell's girlfriend's sister, followed behind him seconds later.

Rell was glad when it was finally over. Though he too was sobbing, he was keeping it under control for Momma's sake. Usually she was the strongest woman he knew. He wasn't used to seeing her so vulnerable, and as the man of the family, he knew that it was his job to console her until she regained her mental strength.

His father's sister, Annabelle, and her daughter, Tara, were among the people gathered to say their final goodbyes. The two of them had come as passengers with Momma in her Mercury Mountaineer, and when they left, Tara was in the driver's seat. They would be following him to his house on Trumbull Avenue for the repast.

As Rell drove the Escalade out of the cemetery and onto Ravenswood Avenue, he heard Tamera's phone vibrating in the black Michael Kors bag he'd bought her yesterday to go along with her black dress and full-length leather coat for the funeral. When she checked the phone and then dropped it right back in her purse, he frowned at her.

"Who was that?" he asked.

"We'll talk about it later," she said.

"Nah. Talk about it now."

Tamera sighed and closed her eyes. When she opened them two seconds afterward she looked at Rell and said, "It's Kendrick, calling from prison again. I blocked the prison number, but he's calling on three-way."

Nostrils flaring, Rell clenched his teeth and turned his eyes back to the road. Kendrick was Tamera's ex. Just over a week ago, he'd threatened both her and Rell during a phone conversation that Rell had encouraged her to have with him, to let him know that she had a new man and wanted nothing more to do with him.

Hardly a minute passed before her phone started ringing again.

She issued another sigh and a roll of the eyes.

"Answer it," Rell said. "Better yet, let me answer it. Give it here. I'll talk to him. Since he wanna talk so bad."

Tamera seemed a little reluctant to hand him the phone but she did it, and he accepted the collect call.

"Look, nigga. Stop calling my girl's phone. A'ight? She told you once, and now I'm telling you. Stop calling."

Kendrick laughed. "I want you to say that shit to my face when you see me, lil nigga. My lawyer say my case should be overturned by the end of the month. I'll be home soon, and I'm coming to take what's mine. Chump."

Click.

Just like that, the call was over.

Rell looked over at Tamera as he gave her the phone back, his eyes as cold as the weather was outside.

"I know what you're thinking, Rell. I need you to stop thinking it. I couldn't care less about that man. He left me a voicemail yesterday saying his charges were dropped or something. I don't give a damn. You're my man, and that's all there is to it."

Rell nodded his head thoughtfully. He hoped that Kendrick would not make him go back to his old ways. In the past, Sincere Jerrell Owens had been a monster in the streets of Chicago, and over Tamera Lyon, the woman of his dreams, he would go back to being that same old monster in a heart-beat.

Chapter 1
February 14th 2016
6:45 A.M.

Tamera had not worn the ring since Susan's unfortunate death. The 9-carat, round-cut white diamond ring was the ring David Owens had proposed to Susan with just four years ago.

As Rell bustled around the kitchen, preparing a very special breakfast for his sleeping beauty, he kept glancing at the ring. It was in an open gray velvet jewelry box on the kitchen table, right in between the salt and pepper shakers, and it shined brilliantly beneath the glow of the ceiling light. The ring gave him all the courage he needed to carry out his plans on this wonderfully frigid Valentine's Day.

Thanks to a culinary arts class he'd taken in prison, his chef game was on point. He had set his alarm to wake him up at 5:30 and he'd gotten right to it, first showering and then heading straight to the kitchen, wearing just a pair of black Gucci boxer-briefs with matching socks and flip-flops. During the several years he'd spent in Stateville Correctional Center, he had exercised strenuously. His build was still like that of a professional wrestler, with bulging muscles and tattoos that covered the majority of his chest, arms, and back. He knew how much Tamera loved to gawk at his chiseled muscles, and since today was all about her, he intended to keep her happy from the moment she woke up to the moment she went to bed.

He cooked a palatable meal of Belgian waffles with strawberries, beef sausages, and mozzarella cheese eggs, made a plate for Tamera and another one for himself, and put them on the serving tray he'd purchased yesterday for this very meal.

There was a clear glass vase with two dozen red roses on the kitchen table. These, too, were purchased yesterday, using his brand-new American Express credit card. He put the jewelry box in the pocket-like opening in the front of his boxer-briefs, placed seven of the roses on the tray, and then headed to the bedroom.

Tamera lay just as she had when he left her over an hour prior, on her side with one leg straight and the other raised at a ninety-degree angle. She had on a red-lace Victoria's Secret bra and panties set, and her hair was wrapped up in a white Gucci headscarf.

The scent of the food awakened her before Rell could do it himself. Her eyes popped right open, and she looked at him through tightly-squinted eyelids.

"Good morning, my favorite jerk," he said, beaming as he sat down next to her and put the tray on her lap. He kissed her full lips. "Happy Valentine's Day, baby. Love you."

"Love you more." Sitting up, she let out a sleepy groan. "Aww, breakfast in bed? Thanks, bae. Happy Valentine's Day to you, too. And thanks for the roses."

A sleepy smile burgeoned on Tamera's flawless brown face. Rell scooted toward the foot of the bed and ate his breakfast while watching her eat.

Inside, he was a nervous wreck.

He was getting ready to propose to Tamera, and he wasn't sure what her response would be. What if she said no? What if she didn't give him an answer at all? He'd seen that happen once on YouTube, and he remembered watching Tahiry turn down Joe Budden's proposal on *Love and Hip Hop New York*. He'd felt embarrassed for Joe, and he wondered if he was about to get the same treatment.

No, he told himself. *Be strong. Be brave. She won't turn you down, and if she does then so be it, at least you tried.*

"Boy," she said, looking more and more awake with every bite she took, "these waffles are so damn fire. Mmm.

And these roses are so beautiful. You know how much I love red roses. Why'd you only get seven of them?"

"Because it's almost seven o'clock. One rose for every hour, to show that I love you every hour of the day."

"You're really pouring it on heavy today, aren't you?"

Rell chuckled. He leaned in and kissed her heart-shaped lips again, then the two of them ate in silence for a minute or so.

"So," she asked, "are we going to stay here? Or do you want to get a bigger house? Have you thought about that yet?"

He shrugged. "I don't really wanna leave the city. If we leave, it'll just be a better neighborhood. I really love the west side, though. Might just stay here. It's a good thing, because we're right down the street from the building."

The building Rell was speaking of was an apartment building that had once belonged to his father, but now belonged to him and Jah. Big Man and Susan had also left five other west side houses to them, and with the money from Big Man and Susan's life insurance policies and the money they'd had in the bank, Rell and Jah ended up getting about $1.2 million apiece. Jah looked at it like they were set for life, but Rell could name at least ten dope boys who'd seen a million dollars, but now had nothing to show for it. He planned to save his money and spend it wisely, maybe invest in a business and purchase some more properties. Eventually he wanted a family, a wife and hopefully a daughter or two, and he knew that taking care of them was most important. He and Jah had not yet spent a dime of the money they'd inherited from their father and his wife, but both of them were running through their fifty-thousand-dollar portions of the $200,000 Tamera had taken from the girlfriend of one of their enemies.

When Tamera finished eating, she got up and took the food tray to the kitchen, then went to the bathroom to get her hygiene together. Rell took the opportunity to take the jewelry box out of his boxer-briefs. He glanced around the bedroom in search of a place to put it and settled on stashing it under her pillow.

He stretched his arms across his chest and did a quick leg stretch, thinking that it was Valentine's Day and that he had to put it down harder than usual before he proposed. He wanted her to remember every single detail of this day. He wanted the memory of this Valentine's Day to be permanently imprinted in her memory bank.

He wanted her to not be able to walk tomorrow.

He lay on the bed, thumbed down the front of his boxer-briefs, and let his huge erection flop out onto his abdomen. He knew that, with his powerfully-built physique and rugged good looks, he was killing the photo The Game had posted on Instagram months earlier. He had not intended to see the picture, but just about every woman on his Facebook friends list had shared it and he'd been forced to see it dozens of times while scrolling down his page.

"I'm crushin' these niggas," he muttered aloud to himself as he gripped the base of his thick phallus in one hand and began stroking it. "Call the law, Tamera. Call the ambulance. Call the coroner. I'm about to murder that pussy."

He laughed at himself, and he was still stroking his perilously large love stick when Tamera appeared in the doorway with her hands on her hips and her eyes on him.

"Yes, nigga," she said, cheesing.

He chuckled arrogantly and nodded his head. "Yep. All this yours, baby."

"All of it?"

"All of it."

She walked to the bed, moving slowly, taking in every inch of him. She was still wearing the red-lace bra and panties set she'd put on after her bath last night. From the waist down, she was nearly as meaty as Porscha Williams, and her breasts were the perfect size — not too big, not too small. Her skin was a rich, smooth brown, the exterior of an African goddess.

"Tamera Lyon..." Rell's chin dropped and he had trouble picking it up.

"Yes, Sincere Jerrell Owens?" She climbed on the bed and moved toward him like a lioness stalking its prey, smiling her flawless smile and regarding his dick with hungry eyes.

"Baby, you are so beautiful," he said when his brain started working again. "Damn. I don't know how I got so lucky."

"You and me both."

"I'm dead serious, baby. You are perfect. Everything I've ever wanted in a woman is you. You do know that, right?"

Tamera ran her tongue from his scrotum up the underside of his long, thick pole, and finally to its head. He trembled when she sucked the head in between her lips.

She took his dick in her hands and choked herself on it, taking him to the rear of her throat until tears burgeoned in her pretty brown eyes. She stroked his length and rolled his balls in her hand, and when she popped her lips off him a minute later she said, "You're not putting it on me this time. Nuh uh. This time I'm putting your ass to sleep."

"Good luck trying."

"Oh, I'm going to do a helluva lot more than try."

She moved up and kissed him. His hands seemed to roam on their own free will, first to the nape of her neck, then down her back, then to her pillowy derrière. He slapped them onto the soft cheeks and inhaled a breath of satisfaction as he felt her ass jiggling in his palms.

He flipped her over onto her back, and this time he did not have to push her legs up. She had grown used to this move.

She pulled back her legs, making her toes touch the headboard, and bit down on her bottom lip as she watched his tongue twirl on her clitoris.

Rell was good at eating pussy. He'd proven it time after time in the bed with Tamera. He loved how good it tasted, how good the scent of it was. She had come off her period just yesterday, and he was all too happy that it had not lasted until now. He'd been starving for the taste of her juicy nookie for five whole days, so it was no surprise how hungrily he licked and sucked on her pussy now, coating it in saliva and holding on to her thighs, pressing his face into her.

Just as he usually did, he sucked on her clitoris until her body could no longer endure the tongue-lashing. She came hard, holding his head and screaming out a moan.

He rose to his knees, preparing to penetrate her, but she rolled out of the way, laughing merrily.

"Get back over here, nigga," he said, jacking his erection.

"No." She shook her head, grabbed him by the shoulders, and shoved him down onto his pillow. "I told you, I'm not letting you kill my shit like you always do. I'm about to throw this pussy on you so good." She was mounting him as she spoke. "You ready for it?"

"I was born ready," Rell said, not expecting what was to come.

Tamera caught him completely off guard.

She guided the head of his dick into her snug pussy and did what she'd only done to him once before, planting her feet on either side of him and slamming down on him with a vicious aggression that left his mouth agape and made his toes curl up in his socks.

The sun was just coming up outside. Its rays shone through the slit in the new gray curtains, which matched the sheets, blankets, and silk pillowcases. An AK-47 with a 75-

round drum magazine stood barrel up next to the dresser. On Rell's nightstand there was a gold necklace with a diamond-encrusted Jesus piece; a rubber banded bundle of hundred-dollar bills that amounted to $9,400; a brand-new 9-millimeter Glock pistol with a 30-shot clip; and an iPhone 6S.

On the other side of the bed stood Tamera's nightstand. On it she had her own pistol, a smaller version of the Glock that Rell had, a rose gold Michael Kors watch, a big blue Michael Kors bag, and her own iPhone 6S.

No matter what they did in the house, they made certain that their guns were always within arm's reach. With all the drama they had experienced this past December, they both knew better than to sit around without being ready to start blasting at any given moment.

At the current moment, however, Rell was ready to start blasting in another way, especially when Tamera turned to the reverse cowgirl position and went back to riding him like a wild bull. Her pussy made gushy-wet sounds. She yelped and screamed and moaned every time her body came down.

Rell wanted to switch positions mere seconds later, fearing that much more of this would lead to an early eruption, but Tamera would not allow it. She kept on bouncing, holding his ankles now. Her creamy juices coated his dick from top to bottom. Her tantalizing moans were like music to his ears. He loved the way her ass wobbled wildly as she rode him.

His toes curled again, but this time it was because his semen was spurting out of him. Tamera continued to ride him. Cum rolled down the sides of his dick as her tight pussy glided up and down it. She didn't let up until he was completely spent.

"Damn," Rell said.

She climbed off him and giggled. "Happy Valentine's Day," she said, smiling back at him as she headed out of the bedroom.

Chapter 2

The snow was coming down hard in Crest Hill, Illinois as Kendrick Robertson walked out the front gates of Stateville Correctional Center carrying a cardboard box full of old mail and pictures and wearing a plain gray sweat suit and prison-issue boots. His beard and sideburns were thick. His head was shaved bald.

Lashaunda was standing beside her minivan, dressed for the winter in a heavy coat and scarf. Their one-year-old daughter, Taraji (named after Lashaunda's favorite actress), was just as wrapped up, sitting on Lashaunda's hip and reaching out to Kendrick with both of her tiny little brown hands.

He gave their baby a quick peck on the mouth and then held his lips to Lashaunda's for half a minute. When he pulled back, he saw that her smile was wider than his.

"I told you they wouldn't be able to keep you in that jam," she said.

"And now I'm right back to the money. Happy Valentine's Day, baby." Kendrick gave her a second kiss that didn't last as long as the first one.

He put his box in the back of the minivan while Lashaunda secured their little one in her car seat, feeling a whole lot better than he'd felt every day for the past year and some change. As he got in the passenger seat, he gazed out his window at the looming correctional center and made a promise to himself that he would never in his life see another prison cell.

"You need to call your old girlfriend immediately," Lashaunda said as she drove off. "She's fucking some nigga named Rell, and from what I hear, he's the man now. They say he's the new owner of that apartment building she stayed in on Douglas. Make that hoe pay up. The least she can do is put you on your feet. I mean, you did take care of her and her sister before you went down."

Kendrick nodded his head. He'd heard all about Tamera's new man from Odella, the mother of his other daughter. Odella's younger brother was a teenager named Zo, who was apparently at odds with Tamera's boyfriend. Odella had told Kendrick everything she knew about her little brother's beef with the Owens brothers, a beef that had resulted in numerous homicides in the North Lawndale neighborhood.

Kendrick didn't give a damn about any of the murders. He had killed twice before, and he wasn't afraid to do it again. He felt like Tamera owed him. Either she was going to find a way to pay, or her boyfriend was going to pay. It was as simple as that.

Chapter 3

Jah came downstairs with a half-ounce of Kush and a bag containing about a dozen packs of Backwoods cigarillos. Ever since their father's funeral last month, all they'd been doing is smoking blunts and playing Grand Theft Auto 5. They had gone shopping a few times but other than that, and the occasional hospital visit to see their good friend Apple, they had not gone outside.

If not for Jah's darker skin complexion and slimmer build, he could have easily passed as Rell's identical twin brother. He had his hair cut low like Rell's, and every now and then, he winced as a pain throbbed in his stomach where he'd been shot in December. He had on a black hoodie over True Religion jeans and Jordan sneakers. The Jesus pendant on his necklace was just like Rell's, only the diamonds were brown where Rell's were white. As soon as he sat down at the dining table, he took two .45-caliber Ruger pistols with extended magazines from under the hoodie and set them in front of him.

Rell had put on a white fitted T-shirt and black sweatpants, and his Glock was hanging out over the waistline of the sweats. He had on his chain. He had his iPhone in one hand and his bundle of cash in the other.

"Where's Tamera?" Jah asked as he began rolling a blunt.

"In the bathroom gettin' dressed." Rell sat across from Jah. "Her and Tirz about to go to the hair salon. I paid for it already. Gon' get 'em the full head-to-toe treatment."

"Man, you be havin' it soundin' like a torture chamber down in this mu'fucka. All them screams and shit. Woke me and Tirzah up with that bullshit."

"Turn some music on," Rell reasoned with a dismissive shrug. He started rolling his own blunt. "We gotta get out today. I'm taking baby to lunch and probably shoppin'. They deserve it after all the shit we done put 'em through."

Jah gave a nod. "Tirz up there gettin' ready now. She got about thirty racks left out of that money from PJ, say she gon' spend a few bands on herself today, and her and Tamera supposed to be going half on a house with the rest."

"A house? Fuck they need a house for? They live here with us."

"Yeah, but I don't think me and Tirzah gon' last too much longer. You know how I am. I told her. She's cool with it."

Rell shook his head. "Lil bruh, you got a lot of growing up to do."

"The fuck is that supposed to mean?"

"You can't make everything about you. Stop being selfish and start being selfless. That girl was at the hospital with you when you got shot. Her and Tamera ain't switched up on us at all through the whole flick. You gotta respect that."

"I do respect that. I ain't changed up either. But you know how broke we done been our whole lives. Now I got a million dollars in the bank, and I got two more weeks before my eighteenth birthday. I'm about to enjoy this money, bruh. Not sayin' I'm gon' blow through all of it, but I'm definitely gon' enjoy it."

Rell was tempted to point out that a real man's responsibility was to build and provide for his family, but Jah was just a seventeen-year-old who'd never had a large amount of money. His reasoning was understandable. He'd have to go through life bumping his head here and there just like Rell had.

"Don't lose out on somethin' good tryna chase behind somethin' new," Rell said just as Tamera sauntered into the dining room.

She wore a skin-tight pair of baby blue sweatpants with a matching hoodie and Air Max sneakers. Her hair was still in the headscarf. The strap to her MK bag was hidden in the fold of her elbow.

Rell's eyes became unwaveringly glued to her legs as he lit up the blunt and filled his lungs with smoke. Her sweatpants could have been painted on. She saw him staring as she went to the living room closet and got her jacket. She looked even more ravishing from the back.

"Damn, nigga," she said, returning to the dining room, "you act like you ain't never seen an ass before."

"Not one that fat." Rell stood and kissed her lips, holding in a chest full of smoke.

She took the blunt and hit it twice. "Me and sis will probably be gone for a few hours. We'll be back by eleven," she said.

"Y'all better be. I got somethin' planned for us after lunch. Just me and you. I don't know what Tirz and Jah gon' be on."

"Shit, fuck them. They'll be good."

Rell picked up his bundle of Benjamins and gave them to her. "That's almost ten bands. Keep your money and just shop with that. Get yourself a nice dress to wear to lunch. And some heels."

"Thank you, Sincere."

There was another kiss. This time Tamera sucked on his bottom lip and pushed her tongue in his mouth. He was six feet even and she was 5'7". She had to drop her head back and lift up on her toes for the kiss. He cupped and squeezed her ass in his hands.

"Sucka-ass nigga," Jah muttered under his breath.

Simultaneously, Rell and Tamera turned to Jah and regarded him with frigid stares. He threw up his hands in surrender, but Tamera chastised him anyway.

"Look, lil boy. Me and your brother are grown. Grown people do this kinda shit. And let's not forget that I was the one who came up on close to a quarter of a million dollars and split it between all of us. Your young ass needs to be loving on my sister the same way your brother is loving on me."

She hit Rell's blunt twice more and then gave him another, longer kiss as she passed it back to him.

"I love you so much, Rell. Thank you for waking me up like that and making my morning so special. I really do appreciate it."

"I love you too. Sexy ass." He pecked her lips. "Go on out and get fresh. See you in a few hours."

He sat down and slapped her on the ass as she walked away. She circled the table and pushed Jah's head to the side with the tip of an index finger.

"Asshole," she muttered as she left out the front door.

Jah waited for the door to shut. Then, turning to Rell, he said, "You better tell your girl to keep her mu'fuckin' hands to herself. You know I beat up thots, too."

"Don't make me fuck you up, lil bruh. It's been a while since I last put these paws on you. I'm startin' to think you forgot how it feels."

"Paws? You Lil Scrappy now, nigga? If you don't get'cha Crime Mobb-faced ass outta here, boa. Love and Hip Hop Atlanta-faced ass outta here, boa. Momma Dee my real momma lookin'-ass boa."

Rell cracked up laughing and Jah continued with the Scrappy jokes for a while longer until both of them were in tears. Jah had always been good at cracking jokes, so good that Rell used to resort to violence against his little brother out of embarrassment when the jokes got too good.

When they finally settled down, Rell said, "I'ma fuck you up, lil nigga. For real." He hit the blunt and held in the smoke for about ten seconds. When he exhaled, he coughed up a storm.

"Rookie," Jah said.

The coughing quickly subsided. "Fuck you." Rell cleared his throat. "You decided on what kinda car you finna get? I'm thinkin' about snatchin' up somethin' for no more than forty thousand dollars. A Camaro, or a Cadillac. Might just go with the Cadi since I already got the Escalade."

Jah shook his head, smoking his blunt with one hand and scrolling through his smartphone with the other. "Nah, I saw a Bentley online for $160,000. Practically new. All red. Might just grab that mu'fucka."

"A Bentley?" Rell said in disbelief. "A Bentley in Holy City? You tryna get pulled over every time you ride past the law, ain't you?"

Jah shrugged. "Fuck 'em. It's legit. I'll show my license and registration and keep it movin'."

"No, bruh. If you gon' get a flashy car, get a Benz for around $80,000. Don't spend that much money on a car. That's dumb, lil bruh. Too dumb. Don't forget, we ain't got Pops around to bail us out no more. He left us this shit, and now we gotta be smart with it. Instead of blowin' $160,000 on one car, you can spend half of that on a car and put the other half on another house. Rent the house out for a couple of years, fix it up, and sell it for a bigger profit. That way you'll make back the $80,000 plus some of the other $80,000 you spent on the Benz. Feel me?"

Jah only nodded and took another puff of the Kush. Seconds passed before he spoke again, and when he did, it was to change the subject.

"That nigga Zo over there on Spaulding gettin' money now," Jah said. "Heard he had a dope line two blocks long the other day. I should go through there and spray some shit up. That hoe-ass nigga tried to rob us, bruh. That nigga kidnapped Tirzah. He done did too much to be chillin' in the hood gettin' money."

"Let that shit go, lil bruh. I told you, you gotta grow up. Stop lettin' lil shit get to you so much. If a nigga ain't tryna hurt me, you, or Dora, ain't no need in tryna fuck him over. And speakin' of Dora, call Felicia and tell her to bring my niece over here tomorrow."

"You ain't gotta rush to get her over here. Felicia and Candace said they're going to Indianapolis later this week. Won't be back until March. We'll have Dora for three weeks."

Rell nodded his head and kept smoking the blunt. He loved having his niece around. Dora was almost one, full of spirit and never without a smile. She made him want to have a baby. If Tamera were to tell him that she was pregnant, he knew that he'd be overjoyed. Especially if it was a baby girl. Daddy's little girl. She would be the most spoiled little girl in all of Chicago.

They finished smoking a few minutes later. Rell put on a hoodie and his black leather Pelle Pelle jacket. Jah put on a similar-looking black and white Pelle jacket, and they went out to the Escalade. Today they planned to go shopping on Michigan Avenue. Rell would buy a few V-Day gifts for Tamera. Jah said he would get Tirzah something for Valentine's Day, but mostly he was shopping for himself and Dora.

The Escalade was an ESV, long and black and presidential-looking with darkly-tinted windows and sumptuous white leather seats. Rell had already thrown six 12-inch speakers in the back.

The two brothers rode off down Trumbull Avenue bumping a track from Twista and the Speedknot Mobstaz, a rap group that they had both grown up listening to.

Chapter 4

"Jah ain't shit. I don't know what I was thinking giving his young ass some pussy. The nigga ain't even eighteen. Do you know that as soon as I got up this morning, the nigga had the nerve to tell me that he didn't think this was going to work! On Valentine's Day! Ughhh, I could have shot him, Tamera. On Grandma's grave."

Tamera was all smiles. She wasn't used to seeing her sister stress over a nigga. Usually it was her who sat around complaining about her broken heart. Now that the tables had turned she saw what Tirzah had been seeing from her for years.

She was behind the wheel of a leased, smoke gray 2014 Corvette that she had gotten shortly after Big Man and Susan's funeral, pulling to a halt at the curb in front of Mariah's Salon & Spa on Chicago Avenue after having just returned to the west side from a downtown shopping trip, where she'd purchased a dress and heels for her lunch date with Rell. The owner of the hair salon, Mariah Janine, was a girl she'd gone to high school with. Mariah had graduated from Paul Mitchell and went on to start her own hair salon on one of the busiest avenues in the city, probably not expecting that it would become the number-one salon for Black women on the entire west side.

"Bitch, if you don't calm the fuck down," Tamera said, staring at her sister with amusement. "Niggas come and go. You know that shit. Ain't that what you always tell me?"

Tirzah's expression shifted from an upset pout to a jealous scowl. "You got a faithful nigga now. Bitch."

"I don't know if he's going to stay faithful. I mean, I hope he does. I'll probably die if he doesn't. Ooh, girl, the nigga's dick game is amazing, you hear me? A-fucking-1. Mmm."

Tamera shivered at the memory of the goodness she'd received this morning. "He woke me up with breakfast in bed. Gave me seven roses. Ate my pussy. Gave me the best dick a bitch could possibly ask for. I almost got down on one knee and proposed to his ass."

Tirzah crossed her arms over her chest and threw herself back against the seat. "Fuck you, Tamera," she said, and it sounded like she meant it.

Tamera put a hand on her big sister's shoulder. "Listen to me, okay? You knew how old that lil nigga was from the jump. If he wants to play that game, then play it right along with his ass. He wants another girlfriend, then find yourself another boyfriend. It's as easy as that. Find another nigga and watch how he reacts to that shit. I bet he straightens up his act in a hurry."

Tirzah didn't look too sure that Tamera's plan would work, but it gave her enough courage to unbuckle her seatbelt and push open her door.

As they got out of the car, they received catcalls from three young boys who were walking past the salon, one of whom doubled back and requested Tirzah's phone number. Tirzah was one of those redbone hood girls with a body like Ashanti. She had been the most sought after girl in school and still to this day, she found it hard to go out without getting shouts from every man she passed. Tamera knew that finding a new man would be a piece of cake for her big sister.

The pair of 7 jeans Tirzah was wearing had her ass looking oh so phat. She curled her index fingers in the belt loops and pulled them up as she walked into the salon.

Mariah and her sister Kia were waiting behind the two chairs at the far back of the opulent hair salon that would seat Tamera and Tirzah, and the other eight chairs were occupied. There were seven more women sitting in the chairs along the opposite wall, waiting for their turns to get their heads glammed up.

It felt good to not have to wait.

"I was just about to start on somebody else," Mariah said as Tamera sat in her chair. "You're twenty minutes late. It's a good thing Rell reserved your seats and paid for the full service, because your butts would be straight out of luck if not for that $2,000."

"Thanks, girl." Tamera reached in her bag, peeled two bills off the bundle of cash Rell had given her, and handed one to Mariah and the other to Kia. "For the wait."

Just about every woman in the salon glanced at Tamera and Tirzah. Neither of them said a word, but Tamera knew they would be talking and texting about her and Tirz soon enough.

To keep away from the fake smiles, Tamera and Tirzah picked the hairstyles they wanted from a catalogue and then focused on their smartphones, scrolling through Instagram and Facebook. A pedicurist removed Tamera's sneakers and went to work on her feet. The manicure would come later.

"So," Mariah asked, "How'd you end up meeting Rell? I heard he inherited some big money a few months ago. They say his daddy owned a bunch of properties around where he lives."

Tamera shrugged. "I don't know anything about Rell's business. He just volunteered to get our hair done for Valentine's Day. You gotta ask Tirz."

Tirzah scoffed and gave Tamera a sharp glance. "Bitch," she said.

Kia and Tamera laughed.

"All I know is that she" — Tirzah pointed a finger at Tamera — "started fucking Rell a few months ago and ever since then, he's been like clay in her hands. She must be suck-ing his soul out or something. I don't know what it is. I appre-ciate the free salon trip, though."

"I'm chopping you in your throat as soon as I get out of this chair, Tirzah." Tamera chuckled. She'd expected Tirzah to go along with the lie, not give up the play.

Mariah wanted the full cup of tea. "So, y'all dating? Not tryna be all up in your business, but I've known Rell forever. I used to live two houses down from him on 13th and Avers, in the house Shanita lives in now. Maria used to babysit us, didn't she, Kia?"

"Mmm hmm. Since we was babies," Kia said. She was brown-skinned like Mariah, just thicker, with a rounder face.

"He's my man," Tamera admitted. "We've been together since Christmas Eve. I don't want to hear about this on Face-book when I leave here, either."

"Girl, please," Mariah said as she began preparing Tam-era's hair. "You know I don't do that. What's said in the shop stays in the shop. But you're leaving out the good part. What is he like in...you know?"

Tamera knew exactly what Mariah meant. She wanted the details of Tamera and Rell's sex life. She was deciding on how much was safe to tell them when Tirzah spoke.

"If you lived upstairs or even next door to them, you'd never be able to sleep. This bitch howls more than a damn werewolf. Wakes me up every day and night with that shit. Either Rell got a big ol' horse dick, or the nigga got razors wrapped around it, 'cause I've been in the house with her when she used to fuck Kendrick and she never sounded like she sounds with Rell. She screams all fucking day in that bed-room."

Tirzah, Kia, and Mariah laughed. Tamera didn't. She hated telling people her business, especially when it came to her relationships. She knew how stories of good sex often led to bitches trying to find out just how good the dick was for themselves, and with the way Rell had her feeling, she might catch a body if he fucked someone else. For the first time in her life, she was completely happy. She had a man who spent time with her, bought her roses, fucked her good, and held her down in every way possible. Losing him would tear her apart.

To avoid further questioning, Tamera asked them to hold on while she dialed her friend Tara's number. She had known Tara since she was about thirteen, but had not known that Tara was Rell's cousin until Big Man's funeral. Ever since then, they'd been talking and texting and occasionally paying each other visits. Tara was the kind of girl that Tamera liked hanging out with, the kind of friend who one could just tell would be forever loyal.

Tara answered, "What up, lil bitch?"

Tamera laughed and shook her head. "Just calling to see where you at, and to see if you had plans later this evening."

"Yeah, the hubby is taking me out for lunch. Not sure where, though."

"Yeah? Maybe we can all go to the same place. Rell's taking me out to eat as soon as I leave Mariah's. You can come and get your hair done, too. I'll pay for it."

"My girl Elana just finished doing my hair, got my shit on fleek. We can probably do the double date, though. Where y'all going to eat?"

"I have no idea. Ask your cousin."

"Okay, lemme call him now. I'll hit you right back."

Mariah didn't give Tamera a moment to breathe. As soon as the call was over Mariah said, "So, how many houses did Big Man own? I heard he had like twenty houses out here on the west side."

"People exaggerate," Tamera said. "I really don't wanna talk about Rell's business. What's been going on with you? I hear you're opening another salon."

Mariah sucked her teeth as if it was against the law to inquire about her business. Then, just as suddenly as her attitude came, it went away, and it didn't take Tamera long to figure out why.

"Yeah, it's true. I've been looking for an investor for it, though. It's gonna cost about $250,000. The bank will loan me about $100,000, but I have to come up with the rest on my own. I've asked just about every person in my family but nobody's going to help me. They don't have it. I really don't see why people aren't busting down the door for the opportunity to invest in my brand. I mean, who doesn't know my name? Owning just ten percent of a salon with my name on it will guarantee your money back within the first six months of business. The rest will be all profit until you sell your percentage back to me."

So, that was it. Mariah knew that Rell had inherited some money, and she wanted to utilize his funds to open another salon. It didn't sound like such a bad idea.

"I'll talk to him about it," Tamera said. "Just get my hair done first."

She ended up getting everything the salon offered — a massage, a chocolate face mask, a mani and pedi, and an impeccably done bob that reminded her of the hairstyle Mary J. Blige used to wear a lot.

She left the salon a happy woman. Tirzah was a bit upset that she had gotten a text from Jah saying that he wasn't going to be taking her to lunch, but it wasn't long before Tamera gave Tirzah a suggestion that made her just as happy. Today was going to be a great day, and Tamera wasn't going to let anyone get in the way of her happiness.

Chapter 5

"I'm about to propose to her, bruh. She's the one. I'ma propose to her with the ring. Susan's ring." Rell didn't look at his brother as he spoke, for he knew that Jah would be looking at him like he was the dumbest man in the world.

They had just left Rev's Barbershop and were now on Madison Street, just passing the United Center. The sign out front said "Chicago's Own Chance The Rapper Live Performance Tonight @ 8:30, with special performances from King Louie, The Real Nixta, Lil Durk, Lil Herb, Lil Bibby, Katie Got Bandz, Twista, and the Speedknot Mobstaz".

Jah waved off Rell's surprise engagement news and said, "We gotta go to this concert, bruh. I know it's gon' be packed. If it ain't sold out yet, I'm about to grab some tickets."

"Did you hear what I just said? I'm proposing to—"

"Nigga, I heard you. What the fuck you want me to say? I think it's dumb as hell for you to be marrying a girl you just met two months ago, but you're a grown-ass man. Congratulations. Wish y'all the best."

Rell gave his brother a tight glance. Jah kept staring out his window until they had passed the United Center. Then he turned to Rell and chuckled.

"What?" Rell said.

"I just think it's funny how life turns out. I used to look up to you for being a player. You used to have so many hoes before you went to the joint. What happened to my big bruh? You lost the swag, big bruh. You ain't the same no more."

"You're right. I was a teenager back then. I'm a grown man now. Responsibilities changed. Give yourself a few more years. You'll see what I mean. If you don't, then I feel bad for you."

Rell was a little angry over Jah's response to the news of the imminent proposal, but he wasn't going to let it ruin his mood. Instead of dwelling on it, he thought back to the morning sex he'd had with Tamera. This put a smile on his face. The way she had ridden him made for an unforgettable memory.

A few minutes later, after tapping his thumbs across the screen of his iPhone, Jah said, "Yup. Tickets sold out. This some bullshit. I'm about to call Big Rick and see if he can get us in."

"Big Rick? You talking about Liffy Stokes's manager?" Rell looked at Jah. "How you know him?"

"He got a baby by Felicia's cousin. Met him last year. He might have the same number."

Rell kept driving while Jah made the call. He drove all the way down to Kedzie and then made the left turn that would take them back to the hood. Like usual, he had his gun on his lap. It was practically mandatory for young niggas in Chicago to keep their guns on their laps while in traffic. One never knew when an enemy might pop out on them, and since there was almost always a gun involved, being without one could mean death.

He was just passing Lexington Street when a 1980's model pearl white Chevy Caprice on large rims came zooming past his side of the Escalade. He squinted at the car for a moment, trying to remember where he'd seen it. He knew that it had been recently. But where?

"We got backstage action, big bruh," Jah said, nodding his head triumphantly as he ended the call. "Fo' said just hit his line before we get there and we in."

"You see that Chevy?"

Jah looked from Rell to the road and gasped when he saw it. He lifted his gun, and Rell remembered where he'd seen the Chevy before Jah even said it.

"That's the Chevy we got Tirzah out of. That's Zo's, bruh. Should fire that mu'fucka up."

Jah was right. They had found Tirzah in the trunk of the Caprice when she was kidnapped a few months ago. He and Jah had not seen Zo ever since that night.

Rell unintentionally caught up with it at the next red light. He looked down into the passenger window and saw a young girl's head bobbing up and down in Zo's lap.

Turning to Jah, Rell wasn't surprised to see an expression of fury. Zo and two of his friends (Chris and E, both now deceased) had tried to rob Rell and Jah in the first-floor hallway of their father's apartment building on Douglas Boulevard. Rell had started fighting with Chris, the sole gunman, and Jah had beat up the other two robbers until the gun Rell and Chris were fighting over began going off. One of the bullets had hit Jah in the stomach, and to this day, the wound still brought him pain.

There was also another reason why Jah wanted Zo so badly. A few weeks ago, word had gotten back to them that Zo was bragging around the neighborhood about how he'd shot up their mother's house on 13th and Avers.

Instinctively, Rell looked around to see if there were any police in the vicinity and found none. But there were a number of potential eyewitnesses. Five cars and a couple of people on the street.

The light turned green, and Rell let Zo zoom off ahead of him. He kept up with no problem.

"Just roll your window down," Jah said. "Ride back up on him and roll down your window. I'll do it myself. Can't just let this kinda opportunity pass. That nigga shot up the OG crib."

In Chicago street slang, OG stood for old girl, one's mother.

Rell gritted his teeth and put his hand on his own pistol. As bad as he wanted to fill the Caprice with holes, he could not help thinking of Tamera and what would happen if he ended up in the county jail for murder. Today was Valentine's Day. He'd promised to make it all about her. But he knew that as soon as his SUV got close enough to the Caprice again, it was on.

As it turned out, he would be able to spend this cold Sunday in February just as he'd planned. Just as he made it to the next red light, a police car pulled up behind the Caprice and flicked on its lights.

"God on that nigga's side, bruh," Jah said as they drove past. "Gotta be God. 'Cause he was outta there."

"It's all good. We'll catch his ass one day," Rell said, and he meant it.

Chapter 6

Somebody started blowing up Tamera's smartphone from an unfamiliar number just as she was pulling into the parking lot at Sharks Fish & Chicken on the corner of Van Buren Street and California Avenue.

"That's his Jag right there," Tirzah said as she looked out her window at Tremaine's sleek green Jaguar.

Tremaine was a heavy hitter on Chicago's west side streets. Tall and brown-skinned, with graying stubble on his chin and a limp to his walk no thanks to a bullet he'd taken to the leg years prior. He was in his early forties, and he'd been trying his best to get with Tirzah since her stripper days. His grandfather owned Sharks, and Tremaine was a high-ranking member of the Unknown Vice Lords who had a bunch of young dealers and gangbangers who sold drugs for him and occasionally shot a man or two upon his request.

"Shit, girl," Tirzah said, glancing at Tamera's smartphone, "who in the hell keeps blowing your phone up like that?"

"If I knew, they'd be dead by now. Go and talk to that nigga. See if he'll come with us on the lunch date." Tamera put her iPhone 6S on airplane mode to stop the ringing. "Don't be afraid to flirt a little. The quickest way to get over a nigga is to find another one. Now go."

Tirzah nodded her head, took a deep, settling breath, pushed open her door, and stepped out of the car.

Tamera looked the other way, toward the Eisenhower Expressway. The sound of speeding vehicles zipping by was soothing to her ears.

Her mind went to Rell. She wondered if he would ever disown her the way Jah had done Tirzah. She hoped not. Deep down, Tamera knew that she eventually wanted Rell to be her husband. At times she regretted taking the ring off when Susan passed away in December. She had worn it ever since he'd shown it to her, even when Susan and Big Man had requested that Rell mail it to them in Miami. Susan had accidentally left the ring in hers and Big Man's apartment before they left for Florida, and she hadn't lived to see it again.

Tamera hoped that Rell had not gotten rid of the ring. He didn't need to pawn it or sell it - not with all the money he'd received from Big Man and Susan's bank accounts and life insurance policies. If there was one ring Tamera hoped to one day be proposed to with, it was the 9 carat diamond ring that had once belonged to Susan Owens.

She turned to watch Tirzah. Tremaine and Tirzah were standing side by side in front of the restaurant. It was obvious that the two of them were being flirtatious. Tirzah kept canting her head to the side and smiling, which was one of her signature moves of seduction. Both of them had their hands in their jacket pockets. Tremaine was smiling so widely that all of his gold teeth were on full display. He wore tan-colored slacks and a black top hat. There were several diamond and gold rings on his fingers. He was as fresh as a pimp at the international player's ball, and Tamera would not be surprised to find that he had attended a player's ball or two in the past.

She took her phone off airplane mode, in case Rell was trying to call.

Hardly ten seconds passed before the unfamiliar number popped up again. 773-555-2212.

"Oh, my fucking God, are you serious?" she murmured incredulously as she swiped to the right and answered the call. "Umm, who is this?"

"You know who it is."

The voice sent a chill through Tamera's bones. It was the voice of Kendrick Robertson, her ex-boyfriend.

"I told you, Kendrick. I'm seeing somebody. It's disrespectful to be calling my phone like this when I got a man, okay. Please stop it. Let me do me. Call the hoes you had those babies by."

"I got out this morning, Tamera. Damn. Chill out. Ain't nobody tryna fuck up your relationship. I just need a lil help, that's all. Who else am I supposed to call? I helped you a whole lot before I went to the joint. The least you could do is return the favor."

"What do you mean you got out? You're out of prison?"

"That's what I just said, ain't it?"

Tamera bit down on the center of her bottom lip and breathed a sigh of frustration. She had intended to hang up on him until he said he was out. She didn't need him coming looking for her and Rell when they were already trying their best to get away from the constant drama that was already haunting them at every turn. Back in December she and Rell — Tirzah and Jah, too — had gone through more than enough drama to last a lifetime. She didn't want to be the cause of even more beef.

"Well," she said, choosing her words carefully, "what kind of help do you need? I really don't know what to—"

"You can save all that shit. I just need like ten grand. I'll give it back to you, but I'm on my ass right now. Ain't got nothin' but the clothes on my back, and this shit came from the joint. Can't be out here letting my babies starve. You know how I get when I'm hungry."

He was threatening her. She'd known him for years, and she knew when he was on some BS. His last sentence had basically been an ultimatum, and Tamera wasn't going to give in. Sure, she had the money to give him. She still had over $30,000 in cash stuffed in two shoeboxes in her and Rell's bedroom, and she was pretty sure Tirzah had about the same amount put up. Not to mention the over $9,000 Rell gave her before she left out for the salon. But that was none of Kendrick's business. He had paid some bills here and there before he went away, and bought her some furniture and a cheap old Ford Taurus, but there was nothing he'd done for her that would warrant loaning him such a large sum of money. Especially since he had threatened her just a few months ago.

"I really don't have it, Kendrick," she lied, turning back to her window to gaze toward the Eisenhower traffic. "You know I've never had that kind of money. Where in the hell am I supposed to get ten thousand dollars from? Damn sure not Dunkin Donuts."

"Don't fuckin' play with me, T. I know what's up. You fuckin' around with a nigga that got long money. Tell that nigga you need ten bands."

"You don't know shit. And don't worry about who I'm fuckin'. If you hadn't cheated on me and had babies with some other bitches, I'd be fuckin' you."

"You gon' give me some money."

"I ain't giving you a goddamn thing. Call your broke-ass girlfriends and ask those bum bitches for some money. And don't call my phone no more."

Kendrick managed to get half of the word "bitch" out before Tamera ended the call. She immediately blocked his phone number and dropped the iPhone in her purse.

"Make me file a restraining order against your ass," she muttered angrily.

Just then, Tirzah came running back to the car wearing a beaming smile. She got in and raised her hand for a high-five.

It was a high-five that she did not get. Noticing the furious scowl on Tamera's face, Tirzah lowered her hand and pulled her door shut.

"He's with it. It's a date," Tirzah said excitedly.

"Great." Tamera didn't sound so enthused.

"The fuck's wrong with you?"

"It's Kendrick. He's out of prison. That was him blowing up my phone. He wants some money. Ten grand. I told him to kiss my ass, I ain't giving him a dollar. Fuck that nigga."

Tirzah sucked her teeth. "Look, we are not about to let that nigga fuck up our Valentine's Day. Tremaine just asked if he could stick his tongue in my ass. I'm getting that today, okay? Now, let's go. Let Kendrick come around tryna get some money and I'll have Tremaine put a hit on his ass so fast he won't know what to do."

Tamera put on her kind face and gave Tremaine a friendly wave as she drove out of the parking lot and onto Van Buren. Her sister was right. Kendrick was nobody to worry about. If anything, Kendrick needed to be worried about Rell and Jah.

Chapter 7

Rell made a stop at the liquor store and bought two big bottles of Hennessy, his and Tamera's favorite drink. Before the barbershop, he and Jah had shopped downtown, where he spent several thousand on a fresh black Armani suit for himself and $1,400 on a pair of Christian Louboutin heels for Tamera.

Jah, on the other hand, had purchased clothes and accessories only for himself. Out of sympathy for Tirzah, Rell ended up buying her a pair of Giuseppe Zanotti heels that were just as expensive as the Louboutins.

At first it had not made a lot of sense to Rell why Jah was suddenly being so cold toward Tirzah. She had held Jah down ever since the day they met, even going so far as to grab his gun and open fire on some guys who'd come to kill him. Although both she and Rell had shot at the guys, he was pretty sure that the bullets she fired had killed one of the men.

When Rell overheard Jah's phone conversation as they sat down at the dining room table, the way Jah was treating Tirzah finally made sense. It was a conversation between Jah and Felicia, his daughter's mother. Felicia was on her way over with Dora, and Rell could tell by the hushed tones in which they were talking that Jah and Felicia were feeling each other again.

He waited for Jah to end the call and then, chuckling and shaking his head in disbelief, he said, "Lil bruh, you ain't shit, you know that? That's foul. But do what you do. It ain't none of my business."

Jah leaned back in his chair, putting it on its rear two legs. "Felicia wanna give it another shot."

"I bet she does. You got a million dollars in the bank, nigga. Every ex you got wanna give it another shot."

"Don't say that, bruh. You know she was with me before all this money."

"Yeah, and she left you. Now that you got the money, she wants you back. Doesn't take a genius to figure that one out."

"If she wants me for my money, this shit ain't gon' last no time. You know I ain't blowin' my bread on nobody but me and my daughter."

"So, you told Tirzah it's over?"

"Yeah. Told her this morning. She was cool with it."

"No girl is cool with being dumped. She might've said that, but you'd be a fool to believe it. She's thinking of a way to get you back right now."

"Bruh, I don't give a fuck. You know I ain't never gave a fuck. She'll be a'ight. She'll live. It ain't like we was married."

Rell knew that there was nothing he could do to persuade Jah to stick with Tirzah, so he said nothing. Instead, he got up from the dining table, fixing the cuff links on his long-sleeve white shirt, and went to the living room to look out the window as he heard an August Alsina song blaring out front. Just as he'd expected, Tamera was parking her Corvette behind his Escalade. He gawked at Tamera's generous curves as she got out of the sports car and climbed the stairs, carrying a Macy's bag and a Giuseppe Zanotti bag. Her perfectly done hair, fingernails, and makeup made her look even more beautiful, and Rell doubted if he'd be able to keep his hands off her when she made it inside.

He'd given her a key the day after his father's funeral. He turned from the window and regarded her with a grin as she and Tirzah walked in.

Rell noticed that Tirzah didn't even glance at Jah as she and Tamera joined him in the living room. Jah stayed seated in the dining room, not once lifting his eyes from the screen of his smartphone.

"Thank you so much, baby," Tamera said, handing him a slimmer version of the bundle of hundred-dollar bills he'd given her earlier. "I only used $3,400. My dress was eighteen hundred, shoes were fourteen hundred, and I gave Mariah and her sister two hundred for waiting on us. Didn't need anything else." She moved closer to Rell, so that they were toe to toe. "I'm so glad to have a man like you. You make my days so much brighter. I just can't wait until the day we get married. It'll be the best day of my life."

"You make me just as happy." Rell kissed Tamera's glossy lips, and as usual, his hands went to her ass. He looked into her eyes and drew a mental picture of how she would look in a wedding dress.

Out of the corner of his eye, he saw Tirzah sit down on the sofa and pull out her smartphone.

"Did you talk to Tara?" Tamera asked.

Rell nodded his head yes. "Her and K gon' meet us at Bavette's. It's a French steakhouse on Kinzie. I've never been there, but cuz said it's a nice place for a romantic date."

"Tirzah's coming, too. She has a date. He'll meet us there." Tamera spoke loud enough so that Jah could hear, and he most definitely heard it.

Jah got up and walked into the living room, face frowned up, phone at his side. He looked from Tamera and Rell to Tirzah. He didn't say anything, but he didn't really need to. His facial expression talked for him. Tamera turned to look at Jah just as Tirzah looked up and addressed him in an even, soft-spoken tone.

"Is there a problem?" Tirzah raised her eyebrows and stared at Jah as she awaited his answer.

She didn't have to wait long.

"The fuck she mean you got a date?"

"She means exactly what she said. I have a lunch date."

"With who?"

"That's none of your business."

Jah's nostrils flared. His eyes moved to Rell. "Bruh, you lettin' this shit go down?"

"What?" Rell scoffed at the accusation. "I ain't got shit to do with that, nigga. That's between y'all. Keep my name out of this shit."

A horn honked outside. Rell turned and fingered down the blinds and saw that it was Felicia in her maroon Oldsmobile sedan. By the time he turned back to look at Jah, the front door was slamming shut and Jah was on his way out to the car.

"Somebody's jealous," Tamera said.

"Two somebodies." Rell gestured toward Tirzah, who was struggling to keep a straight face as she went back to entertaining herself with the smartphone.

A single teardrop rolled down Tirzah's right cheek. She wiped it away before it could fall and said, "Fuck that nigga. Fuck love. I'm done looking for it."

Chapter 8

Jah was furious.

He got in the passenger seat and told Felicia to drive off.

"I need to change Dora's diaper. And I gotta use the bathroom. I thought you said we was gon' spend some time together here in the house?"

"Change her diaper at your house. We can go over there, can't we?"

"Of course."

"Well, let's go," Jah said.

He could smell Dora's shitty diaper. He looked back over his shoulder and saw that his baby girl was sleeping in her car seat, gently sucking on her pacifier, her tiny little fists balled up against her chest.

Just seeing his daughter warmed Jah's heart and changed his mind. He hadn't wanted Felicia in his upstairs apartment because of all the things Tirzah had in there, but after some thought, he decided it wouldn't matter. Evidently, Tirzah had already moved on to someone else, which had him thinking that maybe she'd been cheating on him all along. At this point, he didn't care if she walked in on him and Felicia fucking in the bed they'd shared since late December. His heart was aching from the news of Tirzah's date, and he wanted her to feel the same pain.

So instead of letting Felicia drive off, he got right back out of the car and carried Dora's car seat up the stairs. Felicia trailed behind him with the diaper bag on her shoulder. When they made it into the apartment, Felicia dropped the diaper bag and took off running to the bathroom.

"Go ahead and change her Pamper," she shouted half a second before she slammed the bathroom door shut.

"Man," Jah complained.

He took Dora's changing blanket, diapers, and wet wipes out of the diaper bag. Then he took her out of the car seat and lay her on the blanket.

She woke right up as he was taking off her coat and immediately started smiling, giggling, and reaching up to him. He kissed the palms of her little hands. Her complexion was reddish-brown like her mother's. She was going to turn one later this month. She could not talk, but she could walk like there was no tomorrow.

"Look at my pretty lil baby. Hey, pretty lil baby. You miss Da-Da?" He kissed her lips. "Daddy misses you. Yes, he does."

He got her out of her clothes with no resistance, then twisted his face in disgust as he unfastened the diaper. He held his breath as he took it off. "Ugh, you's a stinky lil baby."

She giggled.

"That's funny to you, huh? I just bet that cracks you up. You gon' have to learn how to walk to that toilet. Daddy can't keep doing this. Daddy's a real nigga. Real niggas don't put up with this kinda shit."

He cleaned her bottom and put on a fresh diaper as quickly as possible. Dora wasted no time climbing down from the sofa and running off to find her mother.

Jah followed behind his nearly-one-year-old, surprised at how well she moved. He was rarely ever around her. As much as he loved being a father, he felt that he was far too young to be sitting in the house with a baby all day. Family life wasn't for him. He liked hanging out in the streets with the gang members way too much to be a family man. Rell, on the other hand, would probably love to be in the house with a kid all day, with his good caking ass.

Jah scooped Dora up just as she was passing the bathroom door, and for some reason, she found it so hilarious that she threw back her head and laughed like crazy.

Seconds later the toilet flushed and Felicia pulled open the door. She took Dora in her arms and headed into the kitchen.

"You still fucking around with Tirzah?" she asked as she snatched open the refrigerator. "Don't lie to me, either. I saw tampons in the bathroom. I ain't no fool."

Jah leaned back against the circular wooden kitchen table and crossed his arms. He eyed the rear of Felicia's jeans. She was just as thick as Tirzah. Not as pretty, but definitely as curvaceous where it counted. Her braided hair sprouted out of the hood of her red True Religion hoodie.

She took out a can of Sprite and turned to Jah, using her butt to bump the fridge shut. "Answer me, lil ugly-ass boy."

Jah grinned. He loved Felicia's attitude. Well, sometimes he loved it. At other times he downright hated it.

"Nah, we broke up," he said.

Felicia's eyelids became stringent slits. She cracked open the soda pop and took a swallow. Dora reached out for Jah, rapidly opening and closing her hands. He took her into his arms and kept his eyes on her mother.

"I would say I believe your dog ass, but then I'd be just as dumb as you think I am," Felicia said.

"I'm dead serious. I told her it wasn't gon' work. On my daddy, that's what I told her."

"Don't start swearing on his grave already. Crazy-ass boy."

"Come on, let's go in the room." Jah led the way into his bedroom and sat down on the bottom of the heavy black blanket. He turned to the Cartoon Network, knowing that it would instantly become a source of entertainment for Dora, and was glad when she fell right into it.

Felicia walked around the room with one hand on her hip, drinking her Sprite, studying every item on the dresser and nightstands, every shoe on the closet floor. At this point, Jah wasn't sure whether or not he'd made the right decision in ditching Tirzah for Felicia. He had broken up with Felicia because of the constant arguments, and they sometimes began with her walking around whatever room they happened to be in at the time, searching for something to argue about.

"So," she asked, still searching, "what made you wanna call me over? You want some pussy? If that's all you wanted, you could've just said that. I might not have worn my granny panties."

"Damn, I can't just wanna see my baby momma?"

"Nope. You ain't wanted to just see me since I got pregnant with Dora."

"See, that's why I hate light-skinned people. You niggas always got attitudes."

"I don't like people period. You included." Felicia was back at the closet, looking down at a row of Tirzah's shoes. There were a few pairs of Louboutins and a few pairs of Jordans. "You buy these for that bitch?"

"Hell nah. You know how stingy I am. I ain't spendin' no money on no bitches."

"Hmm." She turned to look at him. "How much did you get when your daddy passed away? I know you got some houses. And you know me and Dora don't need to be living with my momma and her foul-mouthed-ass boyfriend. You need to get us a house."

"Y'all can stay here." Jah grinned at her, anticipating the scowl and teeth-suck that came a second later.

"Don't make me put your ass on child support, Jah. You know I will. Stop playing with me."

"A'ight, baby. You gotta gimme some time. Gimme a few weeks. I'll find somewhere nice that's close by."

"I'm not moving in that damn apartment building on Homan."

"Did I say that? Stop jumpin' to conclusions and shit. I said I'll find you somewhere to stay."

"And you gon' pay the rent, right?"

Jah nodded his head yes.

"Why can't you just give me one of the houses Big Man left you? I know he owned a bunch of em."

"Because he left that shit to Rell," Jah said, speaking in a defeated tone, as if this was a secret he'd been holding in and not the biggest lie he had told so far this year. "All I got was fifty bands. Guess he didn't trust me with the shit or somethin'. Or it might've been because I'm only seventeen. I don't know. Whatever the case, that's all I ended up with was fifty racks."

For the first time since they had walked into the bedroom, Felicia smiled. She had a wonderful smile. Her pie-shaped face was framed by a bunch of long, thin braids. One of her front teeth was chipped. There was a slender, two-inch scar next to her left eye where she'd been cut during a club brawl a few months ago.

"You know Dora needs some more clothes and shoes. Might as well gimme a few hundred while I'm here, plus a few more since it's Valentine's Day."

She finished off the Sprite, set the empty can on the dresser, and slowly walked over to him. Jah put his hands on her hips as she sat on his lap and lowered her mouth to his for a kiss.

He'd almost forgotten just how good of a kisser she was. Her lips were soft and inviting. He rubbed her ass and returned the kiss, until Dora reached over and grabbed a handful of Felicia's braids.

"Ouch! You lil bad-ass girl!" Felicia shouted, sitting up.

Dora flinched at the shout, then looked from Felicia to Jah and cracked up laughing. He laughed, too.

"It ain't funny," Felicia said.

"Yeah the fuck it is," Jah said.

"No the fuck it ain't." She pulled her braids into a ponytail while Jah's hands slid up and down her thighs. "What's up with the niggas who shot you? Heard anything else about them?"

"That's who got whacked in the alley over there on Avers. Not when Jamie got whacked; the next time, when the nigga PJ got hit up. The other two niggas. They were the ones who tried to stick up me and bruh."

Felicia gasped. "Did you...?"

"Nope."

"Yeah right. You did it."

"On TVL, I didn't do that shit. You know I ain't gon' lie on the mob. I honestly don't know what happened back there. You probably know more than I do. Wit'cho nosy ass."

"Fuck you."

"Stop cussin' in front of my daughter, baby."

"Or what?"

"Or I'ma throw your lil dirty ass out that window." He cast a brief glance at the window for effect.

"Nigga, you ain't gon' do a goddamn thang to me."

Jah hopped up from the bed and lifted Felicia high up over his shoulder as he went to the window. She playfully slapped him about the head and begged him to put her down, while Dora laughed her little head off on the bed.

He put her down seconds later and she lay next to him on the bed, toying with his Jesus piece. She asked him if it was real and he lied and said it wasn't. She told him about her gay sister Candace's new girlfriend and about her mom getting laid off from work as a CTA bus driver. She told him about the cold that Dora had just gotten over, and that last night she had found Dora standing in the bathroom with an entire jar of Vaseline all over her head, face, arms, and hands. Jah listened to it all with genuine interest. He was always interested in what was going on in Felicia's life. A part of him still loved her deeply. He wasn't sure if it was because of Dora or if it was because she had been his first real girlfriend, but either way, he knew that he had a lot of love for her. There were only two girls who could say that they had spent more than a day or two with Jah without being rudely kicked to the curb, and those two were Felicia and Tirzah.

Twenty minutes or so passed before Dora decided to take a nap. Jah covered her with a blanket, and he and Felicia crept off to the living room sofa.

He got on top of her. They kissed. He pulled her hoodie and undershirt over her head and started sucking on the side of her neck.

Suddenly, it occurred to him that he didn't want to mess around and have another kid. Luckily, he had a condom in his pocket. He was ripping it open with his teeth when Felicia stopped him.

"You don't need it," she said.

His brows came together. "Fuck you mean I don't need it? One baby is more than enough for me. What, you on the pill or somethin'?"

She shook her head no, but gave no explanation. There was something about her expression that put Jah on alert. He stared at her, waiting.

Finally, she said, "I'm already pregnant."

Jah's head involuntarily jerked back. "Pregnant? Pregnant by who?"

"Zo. A lil nigga off 15th and Spaulding. We've been messing around for a couple of months now."

Jah didn't know if he should slap the taste out of Felicia's mouth like he wanted to, or take her car, drive over to 15th and Spaulding, and kill Zo like he'd been wanting to do for the past two months.

Chapter 9

Zo had 15th and Spaulding pumping.

His line of heroin users stretched for two blocks. They were waiting for their chance to get a bag or two of the good stuff. Several users had overdosed on Zo's heroin over the past few weeks. Once word of the overdoses spread, more and more customers came.

Sitting on the hood of his white Chevy Caprice Classic, wearing a heavy white leather Pelle Pelle jacket over black jeans and custom made Timberland boots, he was observing the block that had recently become his. Women who just a few months ago had seen him as just another broke ghetto kid were now vying for his attention. Two of them — Zaniyah and Lisa — were standing in front of him, talking about how nice his Chevy looked. Zaniyah was pretty and as sexy as her cousin Tangie had been before she was found murdered in the alley on 16th and St. Louis Avenue this past December. Lisa was a bit on the chubby side and just as pretty.

Although Zo was currently in a relationship with Felicia, one of the thickest dime piece beauties in all of North Lawndale, he wanted to slide off for a night with Zaniyah and Lisa.

"It's crazy as fuck how fast you came up," Lisa said, smiling all in his face. "I know you wish Chris and E could see you ballin' like this. I know they're proud of you."

"They can see me." Zo opened up his jacket to show the picture of Chris and E that was printed on the center of his sweatshirt. "On Neal, I'ma ball for bruh n'em. That's why God blessing me now. He wanna see me ball out for losing my two homies. I'ma ball till I fall and feed the streets like the real nigga I am."

"That's all you're supposed to do," Zaniyah said, nodding her head and chewing on a piece of gum.

All three of them had their hands in their jacket pockets. It was cold outside, but not the kind of freezing cold that warranted shelter. Zo had four workers handling his drug deals in the alley behind his sister's house. His only job was to collect the cash after every eight-hour shift and bring the workers more dope when they needed it. Now that he was getting real money (clearing about $10,000 every day in profits), he didn't know why it had taken him so long to get to this point of seriousness about his hustle. Sure, he was only sixteen, but he'd been in the streets for a long time - long enough to know that money was everything. Nobody got anywhere without it. If he'd have been more focused on getting money from the start, he knew that his best friends would be right next to him, counting big bundles of cash with him instead of being the stiff corpses that they now were.

He figured it this way: everything happened for a reason. God had put him through the hell of losing his closest friends to bring him to this point in his life, and he was going to take advantage of it. Once he made it to $1 million, he was going to give it up and go legit. He had it all planned out. Nothing could stop him, not even a raid by the Feds, because he had his money stashed in a place he knew they'd never find.

The only thing that was really bothering Zo was his beef with the most violent young nigga in the hood.

Here lately Zo had been spending thousands of dollars on guns, extended clips, and ammunition for his team, and he'd even gone as far as starting a relationship with Jah's baby's momma just to get closer to his most dangerous enemy. Word on the street was that Jah was staying in the house on 15th and Trumbull with Tirzah while his stomach wound healed. He knew it was true, though Felicia refused to tell him whether or not he was right. He had staked out the house twice over the past few months. He knew that the black Escalade that had once belonged to Big Man was now the SUV that Jah and Rell used to drive from point A to point B.

His attention shifted from Zaniyah as Lashaunda's minivan came rolling up alongside his Chevy. He looked inside and saw Kendrick, his niece's father, the guy who'd been the man in the building on Douglas and Homan before the law raided his spot.

Zo's first thought was the possibility that Kendrick had been released from prison to work for the Feds.

Kendrick waved for Zo to join him in the minivan.

Reluctantly, Zo hopped down from the hood of his Chevy and told the girls he'd be right back. He got in the backseat and scooted over behind Lashaunda's seat so that he and Kendrick could look at each other as they talked.

"The fuck is up with that thick-ass beard?" Zo said with a laugh. "What up, nigga? Glad to see you out that jam."

"By the grace of Allah." Kendrick instructed Lashaunda to circle the block, then turned back to Zo as she drove off. "What's the thought with the nigga Rell? And his lil brotha?"

"It's a long-ass story, to tell you the truth. Long story short, I ain't cool with neither one of 'em. I really wanna whack 'em."

"What you waitin' on?"

Zo shrugged. "It's too much money flowing through this bitch. We just got the law to chill out a little. A nigga couldn't make a dime in December and half of January. The less murders we got, the more money we make. I'm tryna make as much bread as I possibly can out here. Tryna get like you used to be in the Homan building. I can lay on Jah until he least expects it. Then I'll just have one of the lil homies do it and fall back."

"Show me the house. You say 15th and Trumbull?"

"Yeah. Drive over there."

Zo shook the dreadlocks from in front of his face and looked out the window to the right of him as Lashaunda drove up 16th Street. This was a neighborhood that he now considered his. He was one of the biggest drug dealers in the area now, quite possibly the absolute biggest, and he knew that many of the older guys hated him for it. They had already tried to bribe him into breaking bread in exchange for high rank in the Vice Lord Nation. He wasn't going for it. He was ready to send gunshots at any and everyone over every dime of his money. As far as he was concerned, he was already one of the gang's chiefs. He had guns, he had money, and he had soldiers that were willing to kill about him. He didn't need anything more than that.

He eyed the street as Lashaunda drove down Trumbull Avenue. When they were passing the house where Jah and his brother were staying with Tamera and Tirzah he pointed it out for Kendrick.

"And that's the Lac truck they been riding. It used to be Big Man's," he added.

"Yeah?" Kendrick was just about out of his seat as he gawked at the house and the Escalade. He looked angry.

For a brief moment, Zo sat there and wondered why. Then he remembered that Tamera and Kendrick had messed around before he was sent to prison.

Lashaunda crept up Trumbull at about ten miles per hour. Zo pointed at the Corvette that was parked behind the Escalade.

"That's Tamera's car right there. Brand new Corvette."

Kendrick rocked his head thoughtfully, pulling at his long black beard, his jaw muscles flexing incessantly. "So, they got big money, huh? And the bitch don't even wanna break bread with the nigga who had her living good? Yeah, a'ight. A'ight. We gon' see about that shit."

"Shit," Zo said, "if we can follow them to somewhere that's not in the hood, I'm with it. I'll whack 'em myself. I just don't wanna burn up the hood and have the law out here no more than they already are. Can't afford to be taking no losses."

"How much bread you think they got?" Kendrick asked. "The brothers, I mean. Jah and Rell."

"I don't even know. Probably a couple hundred thousand at least. Big Man left them all those houses."

Kendrick stroked his beard in silence as they turned onto Douglas Boulevard. He seemed to get angrier and angrier by the second. Again, Zo thought of the possibility that Kendrick was out to set someone up. He found it odd that Kendrick was out of prison while the rest of his guys were still in that jam.

Had Kendrick struck a deal with prosecutors to wire up on some local dope boys in exchange for his freedom?

Was Zo on the list of people Kendrick was planning to set up?

Zo lit up a Newport and told Lashaunda to take him back to the block, hoping that he hadn't already said too much.

Chapter 10

Rell heard a scream.

It came from Jah's upstairs apartment, and the scream was immediately followed by several loud thumps and the sound of shattering glass.

Tamera and Tirzah gasped in unison. They had just changed into the dresses and heels they'd be wearing out to lunch. Tirzah's wore a fuchsia-and-white-striped Gucci mini-dress, and Tamera's was a strawberry red one by the same designer. It would be frigid out, but they had long leather coats for the weather. Tirzah's date, an older man in an impeccable black suit and bowtie, had just walked in the door and handed her a bouquet of red roses. Rell was at the closet with an arm in the sleeve of his peacoat and a blunt hanging from the corner of his mouth.

Everyone looked up at the ceiling as the sounds continued upstairs.

"The hell is going on up there?" Tamera murmured.

Rell sighed and shook his head. He'd seen Felicia's car pull up outside. She and Jah were probably fighting like they had done a thousand times in the past. If not for Dora being up there with them, Rell might have ignored the entire thing. But since his niece was the most important little girl in the world to him, he put on his coat and then went to the front door, yanked it open, and headed upstairs just as another loud bump shook the house.

He heard Felicia shout: "Get...the fuck...off me, Jah!"

Rell tried opening the door and found that it was locked. He pounded on it.

"Lil bruh, open up the mu'fuckin' door, man. The fuck y'all on in there?"

"Nah, bruh!" Jah shouted back. "This stupid-ass bitch wanna run around fuckin' niggas, fuckin' hoe-ass niggas who we into it with. Nah. Fuck that shit. I'ma kill this hoe."

"Bruh, open the door," Rell repeated.

There was another heavy thud. Rell turned to go back down the stairs. He and Jah had keys to each other's apartments on their keyrings. He would go and get it and then come back.

He didn't make it down the stairs. Tamera was standing there at the foot of the staircase holding his keys. Tirzah and Tremaine were right behind her. She met him halfway up the staircase and gave him the keys.

"Is he beating on that girl?" Tamera whispered.

Rell did not give her an answer. He simply rushed back upstairs to the door. He was in too much of a hurry to save Felicia before Jah could seriously hurt her.

He heard Dora crying as soon as he got the door open. She was sitting in the hallway by the bathroom door, sobbing and afraid.

Jah and Felicia were in the corner next to the sofa. He was on top of Felicia with his hands wrapped around her neck. Rell signaled for Tamera to grab Dora while he rushed over and pulled Jah off of Felicia.

"Bruh, calm down. What the fuck is wrong with y'all? Get up off this woman." It was a struggle, but Rell was able to rip Jah away from Felicia.

The two brothers fell back onto the floor. Out of the corner of his eye, Rell saw Tamera race out the front door with Dora in her arms.

Felicia sat up slowly, rubbing her bruised neck, tears running down her face, blood dripping from her nose. Her face was as red as a cherry, and she was naked from the waist up.

"She pregnant by that nigga Zo, bruh," Jah said, out of breath. "This stupid-ass bitch done started fuckin' with the enemy!"

Jah tried rushing at Felicia as they stood up, but Rell snatched him back and threw him against the closet door. Felecia dressed hurriedly and silently. Rell could tell by the look on her face that she was hurt, both physically and emotionally.

"You're pregnant by Zo?" Rell said in disbelief. As bad as he wanted to leave her alone, he couldn't stop himself from asking the question.

She didn't answer him. She gathered her things, picked up Dora's diaper bag, and left out the door.

Jah turned and punched a hole in the wall next to the closet. His jaw muscles flexed as he gritted his teeth together. He shook his head and flared his nostrils.

"I should kill that dumb bitch," he said.

"That's your daughter's momma," Rell reminded him.

"I don't give a fuck whose momma she is! She done got pregnant by that hoe-ass nigga! She done had that nigga around my baby? I should've broke her fuckin' neck."

Jah headed toward the door, and Rell grabbed him and threw him back again.

"She ain't leaving with my daughter," Jah said.

"I'll keep Dora with me. You just sit the fuck down so I can talk this girl out of getting your dumb ass locked up."

Jah threw himself onto the sofa, pounding his fists into the soft leather on either side of him.

Shaking his head, Rell went out the door and down the stairs. When he made it back into his own living room, Felicia was putting Dora's coat on. Tamera, Tirzah, and Tirzah's date were all standing around the coffee table, watching Felicia and not saying a word.

"You're pregnant by Zo?" Rell asked.

Felicia didn't reply to the question.

"I'll keep Dora. Go in the bathroom and get yourself cleaned up. Jah ain't gon' come in here. I told him to keep his ass upstairs."

Felicia scoffed at that. "This is his brother's apartment. He'll be down here on bullshit any minute now," she said, dabbing the blood from her nose with a wet wipe. "I don't know why he's mad at me in the first damn place. It's not like I know his business. He ain't my man. If he would've told me, maybe I wouldn't have started fuckin' with the nigga."

"Who?" Tamera butted in.

"Zo," Felicia said.

Tamera and Tirzah gasped. It had been Zo who'd put a gun to Tirzah's head and dragged her out of Tamera's car just two month ago. They had kidnapped Tirzah and attempted to use her to lure Rell and Jah into an alley to murder them in retaliation for a previous killing, but things had gone terribly wrong for Zo's guys and he had ended up being the sole survivor that cold December night, only because Rell had told Jah not to pull the trigger after they had found Tirzah. Zo had also participated in the attempted robbery that resulted in Jah being shot in the abdomen.

"Well," Rell said to Felicia, "now you know. Go back there and get cleaned up."

"I should call the police on his punk ass," Felicia said as she stormed off to the bathroom.

Rell took Dora's coat back off and sat her on his lap. She was still crying. She clung to Rell's peacoat as he bounced her on his knee and kissed her on the forehead.

"Does this mean our V-Day lunch is canceled?" Tamera asked.

Rell chuckled and told her to shut up. He took off his coat and tossed it on the arm of the sofa. His eyes fell upon Tamera's mouthwatering minidress. Her ass looked amazing in it, so amazing that he wanted to walk over to her and give it a kiss.

He glanced at Tirzah, then at her date, then he moved his eyes back to Tamera and said, "So, who's gonna cook? I'm on babysitting duty. The lunch date has been canceled."

Tamera sucked her teeth indignantly and plopped down on the other sofa.

Tirzah, on the other hand, said her goodbyes and left out with her date. Apparently, neither of them were going to let Jah and Felicia's drama ruin their Valentine's Day.

King Rio

68

Chapter 11

Jah left with his head hidden in his hoodie and his hands in the pockets of his leather Pelle Pelle jacket. It was so cold out that his every breath turned into smoke, but he kept the jacket half-way unzipped. He had both of his Ruger pistols in the inside pocket, and he wanted to be able to reach them if and when he needed to.

He walked across the street and alongside his friend Apple's house, across the alleyway and onto Homan Avenue. Then he walked down to 15th Street and started off toward Spaulding with his head lowered against the cold air.

That dumb-ass bitch, he thought. *Don't know what the fuck made me have a baby with her dumb ass. And I know that nigga Zo did this shit on purpose. Let his ass be out here today. Fuck this shit. I'ma whack this nigga right in front of everybody. I don't care if the law out here with his ass.*

Two women who Jah knew were heroin addicts came rushing past him just as he was approaching the alley on 15th and Spaulding. They got in line behind what had to be at least fifty more dope fiends. Jah stopped and looked at two young boys who were standing at the front of the line. He recognized one of them as Roddy.

Roddy was Zo's thirteen-year-old brother - or at least that's how old Jah thought Roddy was. He wasn't a hundred percent sure, and he didn't know who the other boy was. Roddy had on a gray jacket and a skullcap. He didn't look as poor as he'd looked the last time Jah had seen him. He was smoking a cigarette, smiling widely and talking to the other boy.

Jah went back to walking. He went to the corner of 15th and Spaulding and looked around. He saw Zo's car parked in front of a house further down the block, but Zo was nowhere to be seen. Zaniyah, a girl Jah had gone to Dvorak High School with, was walking toward him on the sidewalk. She was maybe fifteen feet away and closing in fast.

"Hey, Jah," she said, all cheerful and shit, as if she didn't know that he was the wildest young nigga in the hood. "The hell you doing out walking around? Didn't you get shot a few months ago?"

Bitch, if you don't get the fuck away from me you gon' get shot, Jah thought, and he almost said it. But he decided not to speak his mind. He didn't need Zaniyah exposing his presence to the others, who had not yet noticed him. So, he said, "What up, Niyah? Fuck you doing over here?"

"Oh, nothing. I was messing around with Zo until he rode off in the van with Lashaunda. That boy been out here winning, Jah. I mean big time winning. Who would've ever thought that his lil dusty ass would be out here gettin' money like this?"

"I'm proud of the lil nigga," Jah said. He was ready to turn around and head back to the alley. He was so mad about Felicia and Zo's relationship that he was ready to rob Zo's spot at gunpoint and shoot it out if anyone tried to resist.

"So am I," Zaniyah went on. Her nose was running. She sniffed and wiped it with the back of her hand. "I think he likes me. The way he keeps looking at me. I don't know."

"Do you think I really give a fuck if that nigga likes you or not?" He couldn't help himself.

Zaniyah sucked her teeth and rolled her eyes. She raised a hand and turned away from him, intending to leave.

Jah grabbed her wrist in a fiercely tight grip and yanked her back to him.

Her mouth fell open. She looked at him like he'd lost his mind.

"Boy, if you don't get your—"

70

Zaniyah froze as Jah pushed the barrel of one of his pistols into her ribcage. Her eyes got wide.

"If I find out you told anybody I was over here, I'm killing you. You understand that shit? On my daddy's grave, I'ma blow your fucking head off. And you know I ain't lying."

Zaniyah nodded her head so hard that her chin slapped her chest. Jah turned back to the direction from which he'd come and shoved her ahead of him.

"Walk," he demanded.

She walked.

Jah followed her until they were at the back of the line in the alley. He stood behind a drug addict and ordered Zaniyah to shout for Roddy. She stepped aside and did as he asked.

"Roddy!"

"Tell him to come here right quick," Jah said, holding the. 45-caliber handgun inside his jacket.

"Come here right quick, Roddy!" Zaniyah shouted, the fear in her voice as obvious as the malevolence in Jah's.

Seconds later, Roddy came running up to Zaniyah, smiling just as widely as he'd been smiling a moment prior when Jah first saw him.

Roddy never saw it coming.

Jah whipped out the Ruger pistol, put its barrel against Roddy's right temple, and pulled the trigger.

Boom!

The bullet dropped Roddy and sent his brain soaring twenty feet away from his already dead body.

The drug addicts fled immediately, and so did Zaniyah. Jah considered shooting her as she ran. It was only a fleeting thought, but a thought nonetheless. He turned and took aim at the boy Roddy had been talking to and started blasting shots at the kid, who instantly fled around the side of a garage.

Then Jah took off running.

Chapter 12

The distant sound of gunshots made Rell and Tamera flinch in their seats.

They were sitting in front of the house in the Escalade, Tamera at the steering wheel, Rell leaned back in the passenger seat ordering a pair of hoverboards on his iPhone. Felicia had gotten herself together and left with Dora just minutes prior, and Rell had decided to try again for the date.

"That sounded close," Tamera said, flicking her eyes over at Rell.

He nodded his head in agreement as he sat up and looked around. "Just drive, baby," he said.

She drove. Away from the curb and up to the corner of 15th and Trumbull. Rell scanned the street, and he wasn't all that surprised to see Jah come running up to his side of the SUV from the alley between Trumbull and Homan.

Jah snatched open the door behind Rell's and leapt onto the backseat.

"Go, go, go!" Jah said quickly. "Don't turn down 15th. Go down to Douglas."

"Man, what the fuck you do this time?" Rell said, incredulous.

"I ain't do shit," was Jah's sharp reply.

Neither of them said another word as Tamera took Douglas Boulevard to Kedzie.

A CPD squad car sped by with its siren screaming.

"Jesus Christ, Jah," Tamera said, breaking the silence. "What in the world is going on? Are you determined to ruin my Valentine's Day or what? Because it certainly seems like it. Tell us what the hell just went down back there."

"Yeah, what she said." Rell nodded his head. "What did you do, lil bruh? What, you went over there on Spaulding and got down on Zo?"

"Close," Jah said.

"I'm not about to play the guessing game with you," Rell said. "Tell me what the fuck happened."

Jah paused. "I caught up with his lil bruh and knocked his shit back. The lil nigga Roddy."

Rell swung around in his seat. "That lil dude is like thirteen, fourteen years old. Why in the fuck would you get at him?"

"Nigga, his brother got me shot and kidnapped my bitch."

"That ain't got nothing to do with it. You're mad that Zo got Felicia pregnant. See, if you would've just stayed with Tirzah, none of this shit would've happened. Dumb ass."

Tamera cut in, "And for the record, my sister is not a bitch unless it's me calling her that, and she's also not yours. She's Tremaine's now."

Jah knitted his brows. "Tremaine? Who the fuck is Tremaine?"

Tamera laughed. "He's the real man who took a little boy's place."

Jah cast a scowl at the side of Tamera's face. Rell chuckled and shook his head. He could see the pain in his brother's eyes. He knew Jah well enough to know for certain that the idea of Tirzah going out on a date with someone else did not sit well with him.

For the remainder of the ride to Bavette's Bar & Boeuf, the romantic French steakhouse where the couples would be having lunch, Jah stayed quiet in the backseat. He was obviously upset. Rell guessed that his little brother was wishing he hadn't ditched Tirzah the way he had. Served him right, in Rell's opinion. Rell knew that it was important for a man to keep a good woman when he found one. There was no way he'd ever ditch Tamera. He'd learned this lesson by going years wishing for a good woman. Jah had yet to learn it.

Chapter 13

Tamera found a table in the back of the restaurant, just two tables away from Tirzah and Tremaine's table. Rell's cousin Tara and her husband were at the table next to Tirzah's. They had left Jah in the SUV. He said he would be fine with his phone, as long as they didn't take forever with their date.

Rell pulled out Tamera's chair for her and pressed his lips to her jaw as she sat down. Then he sat across from her, beaming and studying her face.

She could not stop smiling. Her man was so handsome. His muscular build and Colgate smile reminded her of Dwayne "The Rock" Johnson, the ex-wrestler who she'd had a crush on since she was a kid.

"I apologize for my brother being crazy and almost fucking up our day," Rell said, reaching out to lay the palm of his hand on top of her wrist. "You're so beautiful, baby. I really mean that. You look amazing, Tamera. Like some kind of African queen. My African queen." His smile grew. "All mine."

Rell's loving words warmed Tamera's heart. She tilted her head back and inhaled the sweet aroma of seasoned meats and vegetables. Bavette's was one of those high-class restaurants that Tamera would never have chosen herself. She was more of a Harold's Chicken type of girl. She liked to be around people who knew every rap song on the radio, beautifully flawed Black girls with weaves and attitudes, perfectly imperfect Black men with gang ties and felonies and thuggish demeanors. This was not her crowd. All around her at the other tables were people from all cultures and walks of life. Asians and Hispanics and Arabs and Jamaicans, all here to share a special meal with their significant others on the day that was reserved for love.

A dark-skinned waitress with dreadlocks and red lipstick came over and placed two menus and a basket of bread on their table. She asked for their orders. Tamera said to give them a minute, and the woman left.

"We should come here more often," Tamera said as she opened a menu. "I like this place already. It's...what's the word I'm looking for? Exotic."

"It is." Rell nodded.

"I hope you know that I truly appreciate your love, Rell. You're the best man I've ever had, better than anything I could have ever dreamed of. Everything about you is the best. I don't think there's a better way to explain it. You're just the best thing that's ever happened to me."

"I feel the same way about you," he said. He lifted her hands in his and leaned forward to kiss the knuckles of both of them. "You bring out the best in me. You came into my life at a time when I really needed a real woman, and you haven't left my side since. I can't thank you enough for that."

Tamera moved forward with her elbows on the tabletop and poked out her lips for a kiss. She watched Rell's face draw close to hers. She shut her eyes and felt his lips. His tongue flickered out and teased her, bringing back memories of the way it pleased her in the bedroom and sending a spark through her body that made her lower region tingle.

The ten-second kiss could have lasted a lifetime. Tamera pulled back when their lips separated and gazed into his hypnotic brown eyes. She realized then that there was not a single detail of his handsome brown face that she did not like. Even the slender scar over his left brow was sexy.

"If you keep this up, Dora's gonna have a cousin to play with real soon," she said.

"I wouldn't mind that at all. I actually want a daughter. Or a son, doesn't really matter which. Just a child with my blood in his or her veins, my blood and your blood. My features and your features. That'll make for one fine ass baby."

"I'll need a ring before any baby comes," Tamera said, sticking to her guns. As much as she loved Sincere Jerrell Owens, she wasn't about to sacrifice her life without him making the ultimate sacrifice by putting a ring on her finger. There were already way too many single mothers in the North Lawndale neighborhood, and she wasn't trying to add to that statistic.

Rell nodded his head. "Patience is a virtue." He pulled her left hand to his mouth and kissed her ring finger.

The loving she was getting from her handsome man on this cold Monday had her feeling all warm inside as she ordered her meal. She got the roasted chicken dinner with lemon, rosemary, and chicken jus; elote style corn; and a baked sweet potato. Rell got the 22-ounce bone-in ribeye with mac and cheese, broccoli, and a loaded baked potato.

"This place is too expensive," Tamera said as the waitress left their table. "If we decide to eat here again, I hope it's not until next Valentine's Day. I can't afford this kind of eating." She put down the menu and stared at Rell with her elbows on the table and her fingers interlaced beneath her chin. She looked at the diamond-encrusted Jesus piece hanging from his necklace and thought back to the prayer she'd made to God just seconds before Rell had knocked on her door. "God sent you to me, you know that? I had literally just said a prayer asking for a good man, and you showed up at my door right after I finished praying."

"Believe it or not," Rell said, "I had prayed for a good woman that same morning. I woke up that morning and found out the girl I had been messing around with had sucked another nigga's dick right on the side of my momma's house. I knew she was a hoe, but damn...that was too much. You feel me? I didn't want a woman who would just fuck and suck on anybody. I wanted a woman who would never fuck another man, a woman who wouldn't even hug another man unless he was family. I found that in you. When you opened that door and looked out at me, I lost my train of thought. I was like, 'Damn, she bad as fuck'. But I gotta admit that I was thinking you would be just like all the other girls in the hood. I didn't think you would be as loyal as you were beautiful. You are truly the woman of my dreams. That's not an exaggeration."

"Awww." Hearing him speak from the heart like this brought tears to Tamera's eyes. "I love you so much, Rell. I'll never cheat on you. I'll always be here for you. Always."

They leaned across the table and molded their lips together for a second passionate kiss that lasted much longer than the first one. It was the most wonderful moment of Tamera's life. She kept her lips glued to his until she felt a balled up piece of paper hit the side of her face.

Shocked, she turned to see who had thrown the paper and saw Tirzah and Tremaine staring at her. Tirzah's guilty laugh gave her away.

Tamera mouthed to Tirzah, "I'm fucking you up. Bitch."

Tirzah laughed even harder.

Rell chuckled. "Good thing she did that. I was about to fuck you right here on this table."

"You're so nasty."

"I'm so in love." Another chuckle, followed by a grin. "You know, with the way Chicago is portrayed on the news, people would never think our story was possible. We're really like a real-life Chicago love story."

"Oh, no," Tamera said. "They'd definitely believe it if they knew all the stuff we went through to get this far. It's classic Chicago. Like Al Capone wrote it."

They eased back in their chairs as the waitress returned with their entrées. As Tamera started eating, she thought of Susan's ring and wondered what Rell had done with it. Had he given it to someone in Susan's family? Had he sold it to add to the seven figures in his bank account? Was he keeping it to one day propose to her with it?

She hoped there was a yes for the latter question. She knew how much she would cry if he dropped to one knee and offered her the ring. She doubted if she'd even be able to answer him with a "yes".

Let me quit thinking like that, she thought to herself. *No need in hyping myself up. If it happens, it happens. If it doesn't, oh well. Life will go on. I'll live.*

"Jah almost threw me all the way off with all his BS," she said, looking up from her plate. "First he breaks up with Tirz. Then he beats the hell out of his daughter's mother. And then the nigga goes out and shoots somebody. What's wrong with him? You should take him to get his head checked out."

"I know, right? I don't know what to do with that nutcase. Love my lil bro to death, but I'm not about to keep risking my life in those streets because he can't grow up and focus on what's important. I'm trying to build with you. I'm trying to get my Cosby Show on, and that nigga wanna live life like he's playing GTA."

"GTA?"

"Grand Theft Auto. The video game."

"Oh."

"He's crazy."

"He really is."

"I don't think he'll ever settle down with anybody, but I'm not him. I want you."

Tamera's smile burgeoned. She chewed and swallowed. "You're a wise man, Rell. Very smart. Street smart and book smart. The best of both worlds. Find a way to save him before it's too late."

Rell shook his head. "I've done all I can do. Now it's up to him to take the advice I've given him and use it to better himself, because I got a life to live, and you better believe I'ma live it."

"You planning on staying in that same house on Trumbull? I think we should get out of North Lawndale. At first I wanted to stay, but not anymore. Not with your brother warring with some niggas who live right down the street."

"I was thinking the same thing. I mean, me and Jah make $12,000 a month in rent from the apartment building and those five houses. That's more than enough to pay our bills in a new house. Plus, we can rent out the house on Trumbull and get even more money. I'm thinking about just buying Jah out of the properties, since he don't want nothing to do with 'em. Let him take the money and do what he wants. After his eighteenth birthday, I'm letting him go and do him. It's time for us to work on making some babies and getting our lives together for their future."

"I'm in complete agreement with that." Tamera raised her hand for a high-five. Their palms slapped together.

"Well," Rell said as he stood up, "now that we got all that out the way, let me get down to business."

He got down on one knee and fished a gray velvet jewelry box out of his pants pocket. He opened the box, and there was the ring. The 9 carat, round-cut white diamond ring that had once belonged to Susan Owens.

Tamera gasped and then screamed, "Oh my God!"

People in the restaurant started clapping and cheering before Rell could even get the words out.

"Tamera Lyon...will you marry me?"

Chapter 14

Jah had dozed off in the backseat. He was awakened by the sound of cheers and applause coming from inside Bavette's. He sat up and looked in through the dark front windows of the redbrick building, trying to see what all the ruckus was about. But all he saw was a bunch of people standing up and clapping their hands as they faced the back of the restaurant.

He checked his smartphone and saw that he had two missed calls from Felicia and one from Momma. He was too mad at Felicia to talk to her, so he lit up a Newport cigarette and called Momma back.

"What up, OG?" he said when Maria answered.

"Some boys just came over here looking for you. They didn't look too happy, either. Have you been out here shooting again? I can't take this shit no more, Jahlil. Tell me what's going on. Tell me if there's something I need to be worried about while I'm sitting in this house, because the next time they shoot it up, I just might be sitting here on my damn couch when it happens."

Jah sighed. He almost reached inside his jacket for his guns. He knew that it was Zo who'd shot up his mom's house a couple of months ago.

What stopped Jah from reaching in his jacket was the view of the towering buildings in every direction. Bavette's was located in River North, which was in the heart of downtown Chicago. There were no enemies here, just good-hearted Chicagoans, employees and customers, businessmen and businesswomen, most of them enjoying their Valentine's Day with the loves of their lives.

Jah regretted breaking up with Tirzah. He didn't know what he'd been thinking. She was as pretty-faced and big-bootied as they came, and she had been down with him since the day they met. But no, his dick had wanted more than just her, and now here he was, left with nothing while the woman who was supposed to be his dined in a French steakhouse with a new man.

"Ain't nothing to worry about, Ma," Jah said. "Don't pay that shit no mind. They ain't on nothin'. I'ma go and find out what that was about as soon as I get back out that way."

"I'm fed up with this bullcrap, Jah. I can't keep putting up with it."

"I said I'll deal with it, Momma. A'ight? Don't even trip. I got it handled."

"Well, just hurry up. They're parked right down the street from the house. I think they're waiting on you to pull up, so be careful. Keep that pistol on you."

"Never leave home without it," Jah boasted cheerfully. "You keep yours on you, too."

Jah had bought Maria a Glock 27 shortly after his father's funeral. She kept it under her pillow on the living room sofa, which is where she usually slept.

"I had it in my hand when they showed up at my door," Momma said. "But that's beside the point. You need to stop beefing with every damn body. You already done been shot in the stomach. Don't be having no niggas knocking at my damn door looking for your ass. I should've gave 'em the Trumbull address."

Jah laughed and told her he'd be there as soon as possible. Then he set down the phone and turned up the volume on the Notorious B.I.G. song that was playing on 92.3 as a part of their Valentine's Day special midday mix.

"Now check it: I got more mack than Craig and in the bed
Believe me sweetie, I got enough to feed the needy
No need to be greedy, I got mad friends with Benzes

C-notes by the layers, true to life players ..."

Jah nodded his head to the beat as he smoked his cigarette. The song made his heart ache. He was already missing Tirzah. He couldn't believe he'd been so stupid. And on Valentine's Day, at that.

"I'm getting my girl back," he muttered aloud to himself. "Ain't no nigga just gon' take my girl. Fuck I look like?"

He was tempted to get out of the Escalade and go in the restaurant to demand that Tirzah leave with him, but he didn't want to embarrass himself. What if she refused and stayed with her date? Jah would look like a complete fool.

And who was her date, anyway? Who was Tremaine? He didn't know anybody named Tremaine.

Had she been creeping with another man all along? Had those trips to the hair salon and to the grocery store really been excuses for her to step out on him?

It was definitely possible. Especially since, over the past few weeks, Jah had cheated on Tirzah several times with two girls who lived down the street from Momma's house. The girls' names were Jessica and Tiesha. They were sisters, and he'd been fucking them every now and then since he was thirteen. Both of them were pretty girls with nice bodies. Tiesha was dark-skinned, and Jessica was a redbone. Both of them had multiple kids by multiple men, but that didn't change Jah's feelings for them. They were two of his best friends. He doubted if he'd ever stop messing around with either of them.

He decided to return Felicia's call, if only to hear whatever sad excuse she had for getting pregnant by Zo.

What he heard as soon as the call was answered was far from what he'd expected to hear.

Chapter 15

"He won't let us leave! Get over here and get us now! He's saying you killed his—"

Felicia's urgent whisper was silenced by a flurry of blows to her face and head.

She had been hunched over in the backseat of Zo's car, praying that he would not be able to hear her over the sound of his loud music. She screamed out in pain.

It took her a few seconds to realize that she was being pistol-whipped. By then, Zo had taken her phone and started shouting into it.

"Yeah, I got'cho BM, nigga. I got'cho BM and your daughter, nigga! Come get 'em!"

Felicia raised her head. There was blood running down her face and over her eyes. Dora was screaming and crying next to her, grabbing her arm like the worried little kid that she was.

Zo threw Felicia's phone out his window and sped off through the intersection. He was racing the 1980's model Chevy Caprice up 16th Street. He had forced Felicia into the backseat after learning of his brother's murder, and now she feared that he was going to kill her and Dora to get back at Jah. She could tell by Zo's actions that he was ready to do something seriously evil to her and the baby.

Her head throbbed at every spot where his gun had slapped her. She tried to think of a way out of this terrible situation.

"I didn't have anything to do with it!" she shouted. "Just let me and my baby go, Zo. Please, just...just let us go." She sobbed uncontrollably, though she wasn't as out of control as she was making it seem.

Zo didn't even look at her.

"I'm pregnant, Zo! By you!"

She kept crying, but only to throw him off. A few seconds passed with him not looking back at all. Then he moved the rearview mirror to glower at her bloody face. He looked away quickly.

"Listen, Zo," Felicia pleaded. "You know that I have not been fucking with him. Why are you treating me like this? And in front of my baby? When I'm pregnant with your child!"

There were tears in Zo's eyes. Tears of rage. His hands were tight on the steering wheel. He turned into the alley on 16th and Millard and pulled up behind Dvorak High School.

Fearing that he was about to turn in his seat and shoot both her and Dora, Felicia went back to sobbing uncontrollably. She looked at her hands and saw that they were slick with blood. So was her jacket, pants, and sneakers.

"You ain't fuckin' pregnant!" Zo said as he stopped the car.

"On my baby, I'm pregnant, Zo. I'm pregnant by you. I didn't wanna tell you right away. I wanted to think it over."

Zo began slamming his forehead on the steering wheel, mumbling, "Not Roddy...not my lil brotha" over and over again. Dora was screaming her lungs out. Blood was steadily dripping from the many lacerations Zo's gun had left in Felicia's head.

Felicia had the burgeoning inclination to just grab Dora, open her door, and take off running. But Zo had a gun. She wasn't trying to get killed. The way it was looking, she was damned if she tried to escape and damned if she didn't.

A police car sped past behind them, heading in the direction that they had just come from.

Then the most surprising thing happened. Well, in the notorious city of Chicago, it wasn't so shocking, but it was the last thing Felicia had expected to happen.

Three teenaged boys with dreadlocks hanging down over their dark-skinned faces appeared from beside the school and ran up to Zo's car holding handguns with long clips.

Zo was still banging his head on the steering wheel.

One of the boys tapped the barrel of his gun on Zo's window, while the other two aimed at Zo and Felicia.

"Run that bread, nigga! Get the fuck up out this car right the fuck now before I start bussin'," said the boy at Zo's window.

Felicia was all too happy to grab Dora and get out of the car. As she was stepping out of the backseat she saw Zo finally raise his head to look at the boys.

She did not stick around to see what was about to go down.

Instead, she ran out of the alley and onto 16th Street, cradling Dora against her chest.

A few seconds of silence passed.

Then she heard gunshots.

Chapter 16

Rell kissed Tamera for a long time. Even when they went to a different table with Tirzah, Tremaine, Tara, and Tara's husband Kevin, Rell could not stop pecking his lips on Tamera Lyon's luscious lips. She looked so utterly stunning in her tight red dress, and the big diamond on her finger made her look even more appealing.

Tara and Tirzah snapped pictures of the ring to post on their Snapchat, Facebook, and Instagram accounts. Rell took a picture of the ring and sent it to Jah and Momma. He was just as excited as the others were.

The table they were seated around had a semicircular red leather seat. The girls ordered shots of tequila and threw them back. The guys would be the designated drivers. Tremaine took one shot, but that was it. Rell was okay without a shot of liquor. He was drunk off the love he felt for his soon-to-be wife.

"That's the kind of ring a girl will cherish forever," Tara said. "That big-ass diamond. Round-cut, too! Mmm. Beautiful. Cuz, you are the man for that."

Rell smiled and turned to Tamera, who could not keep her eyes off the ring.

"I can't believe it," she said. "Oh, my God, I cannot believe it. I love you so fucking much, Jerrell. You are the best fiancé in the history of the world. Oh, my God, where are we going to get married? Here in Chicago? Miami? We should get a house first. My mom will fly out here to help with the wedding. I want an all-white theme. Shit, somebody get me another shot of tequila!"

She giggled softly and wiped the tears from her eyes. Rell studied her beautiful face. He was happier than he'd ever been. Since his father's death, he'd been mostly going through the grieving process, but now he felt like himself again. He felt like a good man, the kind of man his father had always wanted him to be.

"I thought you sold this ring," Tamera said, turning to look at Rell. "I thought that maybe you'd given it to somebody in Susan's family. I didn't know you still had it. You're the greatest boyfriend ever. I really, really mean that, Rell. Lord knows I do. I am so, so, so, so happy." She dropped her head back and sent a prayer at the ceiling. "Thank you, God. Thank you for answering my prayers. I knew You'd do it. I left it in Your hands and You cane right through like I knew You would."

Rell contemplated the location of their wedding venue and decided that Miami might not be such a bad idea. After all, it was where his father had spent his last days, and it was a popular vacation destination. He'd always wanted to experience the warm climate. He knew people who'd gone down to Florida and never returned. It seemed like a better place than any to get married.

"We'll figure out the location in the next week or so," he said, speaking to everyone at the table. "If it's in Miami, I'll fly everybody out there."

Kevin said, "My uncle PT flew us all to Vegas when he got hitched. Shit was lit. We went to the strip club and everything."

"Oh, hell no," Tamera said with a laugh. "There won't be any strip clubs. Y'all better go to a basketball game or something. I ain't going for no damn strippers bouncing their hot asses all in my husband's face. No telling what kind of crabs and diseases those bitches done caught. Won't be passing that stuff off to me on my honeymoon."

The guys laughed. Rell shook hands with Tremaine and Kevin. He didn't know Tremaine, but he knew Kevin Earl and the rest of the Earl family from living in the Trumbull Avenue house years ago.

Tirzah said, "I'm the maid of honor!"

"We have to get married as soon as possible," Tamera said, staring at the ring again. "I don't wanna wait. A month from now, I want to say 'I do' and get it over with. No need to wait for too long. I love you with all my heart, Rell. I really do. I'm absolutely sure that this is what I want to do. I don't have any doubts. You're the best thing that's ever happened to me, and I want this to last forever."

Rell wasn't trying to sit in Bavette's and chat all afternoon. He had a few more special surprises for Tamera at home; he wanted to get right to them.

"Y'all, let's go," he said, getting up from the table. "Let the celebration continue at my place."

"I need to use the bathroom first," Tamera said.

Tirzah and Tara said that they were going to join Tamera in the restroom. Rell waited until the girls had entered the restroom to head outside with the guys. He noticed that Kevin had a slight limp to his walk and attributed it to the four bullets he'd taken to the back and legs two years earlier. Kevin, known simply as "K" to most people in the North Lawndale neighborhood, was from the streets like Rell. K was an OG from 15th and Trumbull, and he wasn't even in his forties yet. Rell had looked up to K since he was a kid. He'd been glad when K chose to marry his favorite cousin. Tara was a good woman who deserved a good man, and K was doing everything in his power to keep Tara happy.

When they made it outside, Rell frowned and looked up and down the street.

The Escalade was gone.

"That little motherfucker..." he said as he dialed Jah's number.

K and Tremaine laughed when they realized that Rell's SUV was gone.

Jah didn't answer the phone.

"Ain't this about a bitch?" Rell said in disbelief. "This nigga done took my truck and ain't said shit."

K said, "I just got a text from Perk. He said everybody in the hood saying they think Jah whacked Lil Roddy on Spaulding. He might be on the run."

Rell could only grit his teeth. He wanted to find Jah and strangle him. This Valentine's Day was supposed to be special. It was supposed to be all about Tamera. Jah was making it very difficult for Rell to stay focused on his new fiancée.

Rell and Tamera ended up getting in the backseat of Tara's pearl white Trailblazer. Tamera was so happy that Jah's actions could not upset her. She kept kissing Rell, resting her head on his shoulder, holding his hand.

"Fuck that truck," she said. "I'm just happy for us. Let him have that damn Escalade. We should go somewhere special for the rest of the day. I'm not sure if it's a good idea to go back home. Not after he just killed somebody down the street. There's no telling if they know where he lives. I don't want to be stuck in the house if somebody's gonna drive by and shoot it up. You see what Zo did to your mom's house. I'm quite sure he'll do it to ours, too, especially since his brother has been killed."

"Jah is so fucking stupid." Rell shook his head.

"Don't let it get to you. We're okay. We're together. That's all that counts."

"I know, but it's still frustrating. He never listens. I want him to win. I want him to do something positive. He got all that fucking money and he's out here acting like O-Dog from *Menace to Society*. It's ridiculous."

Rell took a moment to settle down. The blunt K fired up helped. He dialed his mother's number and listened as she told him that some guys had come to her house looking for Jah. He told Momma to get out of there and go to the hotel of her choice. He would meet her there and pay for the room. She chose the W Hotel, and Rell told Tara to stop by there before they headed home.

Tamera interlaced the fingers of her left hand with his right one and said, "Everything is going to be just fine. Leave it all in God's hands. You see how far He's brought us. With the faith of a mustard seed you can move mountains. Don't forget that."

Rell turned to his beautiful queen. He looked down at the ring and then raised his eyes back to her pretty brown face. He grabbed her by the underside of her chin and pressed his lips to hers.

"You're what I needed, Tamera. I swear on everything I love, you're what my life has been missing."

"Same here, my sexy man."

"Don't call me sexy."

Tamera laughed. "What? You are sexy."

"No. I'm not sexy."

"Yes, you are."

"I'm a real nigga. I ain't got no swag or none of that gay-ass shit. I'm just me. I'll take handsome, but I can't go for sexy."

Tamera rolled her eyes and shook her head. "Whatever, boy." She kissed him on the cheek. "You're sexy to me. You'll always be my sexy man. Doesn't matter what you think about it."

She spent a few moments studying the ring. Its round-cut diamond was 9 carats of flawless bling. Its band was covered in crushed white diamonds. The way it sparkled in the sunlight made Rell smile. His heart swelled in his chest. He had done it. He had proposed to the woman of his dreams and she'd said yes. He now had the most beautiful woman he'd ever dated locked in for marriage, and he could not have been happier.

When they made it to the W Hotel on Lake Shore Drive, he got out and opened Tamera's door like the gentleman he was. He grazed a hand over her big, soft ass and wished they were alone so that he could take advantage of the dress she wore under the long black leather coat.

"We should just stay here," Tara said.

K said that maybe he would stay if he had the money, and since Rell had it, he volunteered to pay for their room just as Tremaine's green Jaguar pulled up behind the Trailblazer.

In the lobby, he had the girls take a seat while he and the guys went to the information desk. A skinny white woman with thin-framed glasses and a modest ponytail looked up at Rell from behind the desk. Her smile could not have been drawn more perfectly. She had one of those smiles that made everyone who saw it smile.

Rell smiled. "Good afternoon, ma'am. My friends are looking to get three romantic suites. Maybe with red rose petals on the bed and in the bathtub, if that's at all possible.

"Sweetie, this is the W. Anything is possible. Hold one moment please." She picked up the phone on her desk and dialed a number.

Rell turned to Tremaine and K.

"This is nice," K said, looking around at all the sophisticated artwork and designs that made up the hotel's recently renovated lobby.

K was the type of light-skinned guy that made you wonder if he was half white. His brothers, Cory, Joseph, and Antonio, were all dark-skinned. He was the only high yellow child his parents had birthed.

"It really is," Rell agreed. "I hadn't planned on spending any time in a hotel today, but I'm glad it's this one. She said they got romantic suites, too. Perfect."

"I bet the rooms are expensive as hell," K said. "If it's too expensive, I'm good. I wouldn't even do you like that, Cuz."

Rell gave K a look of incredulity. "Come on, now, cousin. It's Valentine's Day. I know you and Tara wanna enjoy it. It ain't nothing. I got it."

Tremaine nodded his head. "I'll throw in a few hundred for y'all, too. We can turn this bitch up together. Be like *Hangover* part four."

Rell and K laughed. Tremaine chuckled and took a thick knot of cash out of his pocket. He peeled off five hundred-dollar bills and handed them to K.

"We gon' kick it like grown folks," Tremaine said.

"Most definitely." Rell pulled out his own bundle of hundred and gave K another $500. "That's on me. I'm still paying for the room, too. Just have fun, big cousin. We gotta make this day special for the queens."

"For real," Tremaine said. "I'm trying to suck that pussy so good that lil momma never even thinks about leaving my side. Been after her for about ten years. She was the coldest piece I saw out west back then and she still is. All that ass. Don't make no fucking sense."

Rell had to laugh again as he turned back to the receptionist. He paid with his American Express card. Two suites for just over $300 each. Both were now being decorated with red rose petals from the door to the bed to the bathtub. Tremaine paid cash for his room. The receptionist said that their rooms would be ready within the next twenty minutes. Rell nodded, added two bottles of Hennessy and champagne to the order, and thanked her before he and the guys headed over to the girls.

Tamera was sitting between Tirzah and Tara. Rell leaned forward with his hands on her knees and kissed her lips. Their tongues danced. He loved seeing her so happy, and knowing that it was because of his proposal to her warmed his heart.

"They're getting our room ready now," he said.

"Is it the presidential suite?"

"I don't know. It's three hundred dollars a night. Better come with a visit from President Obama for that kinda money."

"Oh, shut up. El Cheapo."

"I ain't cheap. I'm just smart with my money."

"In other words you're a fucking cheapskate. You'd better have us some good wine or champagne."

"If you think I'm about to drink some wine, you're smoking the best crack in the city."

"There's nothing wrong with drinking wine. It's all Olivia Pope drinks on *Scandal*."

"Do I look like Olivia—"

"Shut the hell up, Rell. Give me another one of those juicy kisses."

"I wanna kiss on those other lips," Rell said, biting down on the center of his bottom lip.

"Oh, really?" Tamera's eyebrows lifted. She mimicked his lip-bite. "We need to hurry up and get to that room then, huh?"

"The quicker the better. They said twenty minutes. Can you wait that long?"

Tamera sighed and pouted, crossing her arms over her chest, as if it would literally kill her to wait for such a short time.

"We need to talk about our wedding," she said.

Rell shook his head no. "Not today. Today we'll celebrate our love and our engagement. We can get all the wedding details figured out in the next few weeks."

"Yeah, but we can at least estimate how much we're going to spend on it? I think fifty grand is good. Maybe a little more."

"I think you're a little more than crazy if you think I'm spending that much money on a wedding."

Tamera laughed. "You can be El Cheapo all you want any other day, but not for our wedding day. That's my day."

"Our day. I have some kind of say in how much we spend."

"I'll spend ten grand of my own money," she said.

"Then we should have a twenty-thousand-dollar wedding."

"Ugh. I cannot stand you right now." Tamera twisted her expression in disgust and shoved Rell's face away from her. "Keep it up and you're gonna be fucking yourself in that room."

Rell's eyes got wide. He cocked his head to the side and looked at her to see if she was playing with him. She seemed too serious for his liking, so he folded.

"Okay, baby. A fifty-thousand-dollar wedding it is. We cool now?"

Tamera showed him a smirk and shook her head. "That's a damn shame. Your horny ass. Is that all I have to do to get you to cave? Threaten not to give you sex?"

"You'll get me every time," Rell admitted with a chuckle.

Just as promised, twenty minutes passed before the receptionist came over and told Rell that the rooms were ready. He thanked her and then held Tamera's hand as she stood up from the chair, gawking at her stunningly beautiful features in a way that was similar to the way a lion might eye a zebra before he ate it alive.

As they were waiting for the elevator door to open, he said, "I hope you know that it's about to be the exact opposite of what went down this morning."

Tamera rolled her eyes.

The elevator door opened, and they all stepped in.

Chapter 17

Jah didn't answer his phone when Rell called because he was far too focused on saving Dora, and he knew that Rell would only chastise him for taking the Escalade without telling anyone.

"This was supposed to be mine, anyway," Jah muttered vacantly as he raced toward his west side neighborhood.

His teeth were clenched tight together. His two .45-caliber handguns were next to him on the passenger seat. He kept twisting his tightly gripping hands on the steering wheel and rocking back and forth, not to Young Jeezy's "Gold Bottles" song that was playing from the speakers, but to his own beat.

"ARs over here, they pop like gold bottles
47s over here, they pop like gold bottles
Ain't no bitches in the section, you got no bottles
Nigga, we winnin' over here, we poppin' gold bottles..."

Jah veered onto Kedzie and immediately picked up one of his guns.

"On Vice Lord, if this nigga done hurt my daughter..." Jah was angrier than he'd been earlier after learning of Felicia's pregnancy.

He made it to 16th Street without incident but then he had to slow down; there were police cars coming and going in both directions, and he wasn't trying to be sitting in jail while Zo had Dora. Jah didn't really care what happened to Felicia. It was Dora he was worried about.

The Jeezy song did not fit Jah's mood, but he didn't change it because lately he'd grown used to listening to the *Church in These Streets* album.

He thought that perhaps Chief Keef or Lil Durk would be best to fit his current mood. He was in the mood to start shooting until the extended magazines in his guns were depleted.

He turned onto Spaulding and cruised past the house where he knew Zo's sister lived. Since Zo's Chevy Caprice was nowhere to be seen, he assumed that Zo, too, was gone. There were several police cars parked along the street, and when he made it to 15th and looked toward the alley where he'd shot Roddy, he saw yellow crime scene tape and three more CPD vehicles.

He circled back around to 16th Street and drove past Spaulding this time, his eyes flicking in every direction, searching for the white Caprice.

"Where you at, lil nigga?" he mumbled, realizing at this point that he was ready and willing to gun down Zo right in front of the police if he had to.

16th Street was practically a barren land of ramshackle businesses, drug-dealing gang members, and vacant lots. Decades ago, North Lawndale had been a thriving strip of Black-owned businesses (Jah had watched a documentary about it after getting fed up with the conflicting stories he heard from older guys in the neighborhood). Now, though, the strip was so drug-infested that one could find empty dope baggies on just about every corner. Police and federal agents raided spots in the neighborhood at least twice every season. Gang-related homicides occurred so regularly that most of the living population wore shirts to represent the deceased young soldiers.

Though Jah had been born and raised on 13th and Avers, he knew most of the people who lived around here, too. In the past, he'd stayed the night at a dozen homes around here. He knew everyone from the high-ranking gang leaders to the grimy young gangbangers.

His eyes widened in shock when he made it to Trumbull Avenue.

An older woman was helping Felicia into a gray Buick that was parked a couple of feet from the corner. Felicia had blood all over her. The older woman was holding Dora.

Jah veered over and parked right behind the Buick. Felicia must have glanced back and saw him because she got right back out of the Buick, grabbed Dora from the woman, and came running to the Escalade. He put his guns on his lap as Felicia got in next to him.

Upon closer inspection, Jah saw that there were several knots on Felicia's head, including one over her left eyebrow that looked like it needed some serious medical attention. Dora was also covered in blood, and she looked like she'd been crying a lot.

Jah tucked the pistols in the pocket on his door and pulled Dora onto his lap. He reversed and then turned down Trumbull Avenue.

"You might wanna park in the garage if you're going to the house on Trumbull," Felicia said. "He knows where you live. He kept driving past looking for this truck. Oh, my God, Jah, I thought I was dead. I thought he was going to kill me."

Jah nodded but said nothing. He kissed Dora on the forehead and held his lips there as if his baby girl would die if he didn't love on her enough at this very moment.

He did as Felicia suggested and drove around to the alley and into the garage behind the Trumbull Avenue home. Once inside the garage, he got out and pulled down the sliding door before rejoining Felicia in the SUV.

"Zaniyah told him everything. She said that she saw you shoot Roddy," Felicia said, using one of Dora's wet wipes to clean the blood from her face. "This shit is too much for me, Jah. I'm taking my baby and getting the fuck away from this shit. I didn't know you and Zo had beef. Shit. Nobody told me. Nobody fucking told me. I should have been warned. Now I'm wondering if his whole mission was to fuck me to get closer to you. I'm starting to understand why he was asking about you. The nigga was on bullshit the whole time."

"I'ma blow his head off, too. He gon' die like his brother died. Ol' bitch ass nigga should've been dead." Jah's teeth were clenched again. He gave Dora another kiss to the forehead. "Where did he go?"

"Some niggas on Millard tried to jack him, right behind Dvorak. I got out and ran. I heard some gunshots, but I didn't look back to see what happened. I just kept running up 16th. My mind was on making sure Dora was safe. Fuck, Jah. Look at my face. He beat the shit out of me."

Jah nodded his head. "Want me to take you to the hospital?"

"No," Felicia said. "Let's just go somewhere safe. I don't wanna be here when he's looking for you. There's no telling who else he has looking for you."

"Let's get you cleaned up first," Jah said. "After that we can leave. We can go wherever you wanna go. I got my American Express card and my bank card. We'll be straight. I'll get you situated and then we can be on our way."

Reluctantly, Felicia agreed to his stipulations. He let her carry Dora inside while he trudged through the snow behind her, holding both of his pistols and looking around to make sure no one was going to hop out and start spraying.

They made it inside, and Felicia sat Dora on the kitchen table while Jah went and got the first aid kit from the bathroom. He cleaned her up good. She had a couple of cuts and knots on her scalp, but for the most part she was okay. Nothing an ice pack and a few Band-Aids couldn't fix.

Jah regretted putting his hands on Felicia. Not only was he setting a bad example for Dora, he was also hurting Dora's mother, something that Dora might grow up and hate him for.

"I'm sorry," he said, gazing into Felicia's eyes as he put a bag of ice on the knot over her brow. "I overreacted. It's just that I hate that lil nigga so much. He tried to rob me, and he was really planning to whack me when he snatched up Tirzah in December. Plus, he shot up Momma's house. I wanna put that nigga under the earth for that shit. You know how I get down. I can't go. I'ma whack that nigga soon's I catch him."

"I know, Jahlil." Felicia sighed. "You need a good woman in your life. I know that things won't ever work out between us. You're stupid for letting Tirzah go. She held your ass down, and she's about that life. Every nigga around here wants to fuck with her, and she turns them all down because she's with you. One of the boys on my block has been trying to get at her for a while. His name's Shondale. He keeps telling her to stop fucking around with little boys, because of your age. He's in his early thirties."

"Fuck that hoe-ass nigga," Jah said, suddenly angry again. "And fuck Tirzah, too. That bitch ain't shit."

"You don't mean that. She's a bad bitch, Jahlil. You know it like I know it. I'd rather see you with her than with any of these other thot bitches around here. At least she's a bad bitch who ain't running around fucking any and every-body like the rest of these hoes. I was really surprised that you called me this morning. I thought you and her would be spending the day together."

"I ain't thinking about that bitch," Jah said as he walked to the refrigerator, thinking about Tirzah.

He wanted to kill whoever Tirzah's date was right in front of her to show her that she was his and only his. He couldn't believe that, after almost two months of being with her 24/7, she had moved on so quickly the very first time he broke up with her. It made him feel like she had never wanted him in the first place, like she had been waiting on an opportunity to leave him.

"Why'd you break up with her?" Felicia asked.

Jah shrugged his shoulders. He poured a bottle of apple juice for Dora and gave it to her before sitting down next to Felicia.

"I don't know," he said. "Sometimes I do dumb shit. I ain't no different from anybody else. I ain't perfect. I wasn't thinking."

"You really need to stop doing that kind of dumb shit. You're almost eighteen. It's time to grow up. Stop acting like a spoiled little boy. You're a grown-ass man, Jahlil. Start acting like it."

Jah could only nod his head. Felicia was right, and he knew it. He had fucked up yet again. Tirzah was the best thing that had ever happened to him, and he'd blown it for no reason other than the fact that he wanted to party with other women with the money he'd gotten from his father's life insurance policies.

"After you drop me off," Felicia said, "you need to go and find that girl. Admit that you were wrong and ask her to forgive you. Beg her if you have to. Whatever it takes to get her back, do it. Because if there's one thing I know for sure it's that a good woman like Tirzah is harder to find in the hood than a needle in a haystack."

Chapter 18

Tamera's heart skipped a beat as Rell pushed open the door to their hotel suite.

There was a trail of rose petals leading from the door and into the room. Rell took off her coat for her, and then she turned to face him as he shut the door.

He was biting down on the middle of his bottom lip again. He put his hands on her ass and slipped them under her dress.

"Happy Valentine's Day, my queen. I love you more than I've ever loved anything in the world. I'm willing to change and better myself for you. I wanna give you the world. You're my better half, and I want you by my side until my very last day on earth."

His heartfelt words brought tears to Tamera's eyes. He kissed her, softly. He led her past a king size bed that had rose petals in the shape of a heart on the blanket and to the bathroom. The bathtub was full of steaming hot water that was covered in red rose petals. Five scented candles were spaced along the tub's ledge, as well as an ice-filled bucket that held a bottle of Belaire Rosé champagne and a bottle of Hennessy.

"Go ahead and get in the tub," Rell said, turning to leave. "I'll be right back."

Tamera let out a big sigh of happiness as Rell left the bathroom. She studied the gray marble sink, and the bidet next to the toilet, and her reflection in the spotless mirror. She extended her left hand toward the mirror and looked at the engagement ring's reflection.

"God did that," she said to herself, and she had to force down a scream of excitement. "Yes You did, Lord. You showed up and showed out! Won't You do it!"

She kicked off her heels and peeled off the dress, feeling better than she'd ever felt before. Her hair was done up so perfectly that she contemplated sending Mariah another hundred dollars for the good work.

When Rell returned with two crystal stem glasses for the champagne, Tamera was already in the tub. He stood at the sink and popped open the champagne. He had taken off his pea coat and suit jacket. All he wore now was a white button-up shirt and his slacks.

"You're going to be the greatest husband," Tamera said, regarding him with googly eyes as he turned to face her and handed her a glass of the bubbly. "I am so serious. I feel it in my heart, Rell. I really do."

"I'll do my best." He leaned back on the sink and sipped. "My pops always told me that a man ain't complete until he finds his wife. All the street niggas I know calmed down once they got married. I used to think I would never find a woman good enough to marry, and I thought that if I did so happen to find her, I wouldn't be good enough for her. I know that probably sounds crazy, but it's the truth."

Tamera stared at her fiancé. A couple of seconds of silence passed. He unbuttoned his shirt, took it off, and tossed it onto a hook next to the shower door.

His abdominal muscles were chiseled to perfection. It was evident that he had done thousands of sit-ups during his stint in prison. By the looks of his chest and arms, thousands of pullups and pushups had also been a part of his daily routine.

She could see the print of his manhood in his pants. It leaned slightly to the left, and it was long and fat, even when it wasn't erect. The sight of it made Tamera's mouth water. Knowing that it was all hers made her heart skip another beat.

"Stop looking at my dick like that, you lil pervert." Rell laughed.

Tamera looked up at his face, smiling sheepishly. "Remember the way you fucked me that one night at your mom's house? Right before it went down in the alley?"

"How could I forget?"

"I want you to do me like that. Eat my pussy just enough to set me on fire, then put that big boy in me and beat it up until you make tears come out of my eyes. Make me scream your name. That's what I want from you this time. Is that too much to ask? Can you handle that?"

"Your wish is my command."

"Okay, now. Don't say that and tap out like you did this morning."

"Tap out?" Rell's lips moved to the side. "Who tapped out? I didn't tap out."

"Sure you didn't."

"I didn't, nigga. I'm man enough to admit if I did any tapping out. I didn't submit, and I never will."

Tamera rolled her eyes and finished off her champagne. She washed herself in slow, circular motions. Rell watched in silence with an unmistakable lust in his sweet brown eyes. He poured himself another glass of the bubbly and sipped it slowly, biting his lower lip every time she touched her breasts.

The bulge in his pants grew larger and larger as the minutes passed. He adjusted it a few times, then finally took off his pants and put them on the hook with his shirt.

His dick was fully erect. Tamera ogled it like she'd never seen it before. It poked so far out from his waist that it stretched his black boxer briefs to the limit. He grabbed it in one hand and drank his champagne with the other, staring at Tamera as if he was getting ready to hop in the tub with her.

"That motherfucker hurts me sometimes, you know that?" she said, unable to look away from the print in his underwear. "Sometimes, it feels like you're tearing something up inside me. Mmm, but it feels so good! If there's any kind of pain I can take all day and night, it's that kind of pain."

Shaking his head and chuckling to himself, Rell left the bathroom again. "Hurry up," he shouted.

Seconds later, the smooth sounds of a J. Cole song drifted into the bathroom and made Tamera even thirstier for the good pain Rell had been giving her since this past Christmas Eve.

"I want it bad, and I ain't never been obsessed before
She wrote a note that said 'You ever had sex before?'
Damn.
And I ain't never did this before, no
And I ain't never did this before, no..."

Tamera came walking out of the bathroom wearing nothing but her Christian Louboutin heels under a fluffy white bathrobe. Rell was doing pushups near the foot of the bed. He laughed when he looked up and saw her standing over him.

"Was getting my arms and chest right," he explained, getting to his feet. "Shit swells up when I work out a little."

"You're already buff enough for me, baby," Tamera said. She walked to him and hopped up, wrapping her legs around his waist. She immediately felt his steel-hard pole on her pussy.

"You ready to give me my Valentine's Day present?" she asked.

Rell threw her to the bed and hopped on top of her. He sucked her bottom lip into his mouth and then said, "I think the better question is, are you ready?"

Chapter 19

She tasted sweeter than any candy, smelled better than any fragrance. Her moans sent chills through his skin as he drummed his tongue on her clitoris and penetrated her snug opening with two fingers. With his free hand he roamed her curves, from her meaty thigh to her wide hip and finally up to her perky breasts. He grazed the palm of his hand over her slender waistline. She had a belly ring that looked extra sexy from his vantage point between her thighs.

"Oh, my God...Rell...please don't stop...mmm." She ran her fingers through his low-cut hair. Her body trembled as he sucked on her clit like a baby nursing a bottle.

Her moans were like music to his ears.

The room had a mostly white décor: white sheets, a white blanket, white silk pillowcases, white stucco walls, and an L-shaped white leather sofa that ran along the wall from the head of the bed to the large window next to it. The window had a snow-white sliding curtain, and it was pulled open, allowing the sunlight to fill the room with its glorious glow. Across from the foot of the bed there was a wall-mounted wide screen smart television over a glass-topped marble desk. The TV was equipped with the internet. Rell had selected the J. Cole station on Pandora.

As always, Rell's Glock pistol was not far away. It lay on the sofa next to his iPhone and his bundle of hundred-dollar bills, looking strangely out of place in the lavish hotel room. His shoes were on the floor next to the desk. The only items of clothing he had on were his socks and boxer briefs.

For one fleeting moment, Rell thought of Jah and wondered what his little brother was up to. He figured it had to be serious for Jah to just taken off in the SUV without telling him.

He hoped everything was okay, and that Jah wasn't somewhere shooting again. With Jah, it was certainly possible.

The thoughts of Jah left just as quickly as they came when Tamera started winding her hips and digging her fingernails into Rell's scalp. He spit on her pussy and then slurped up the juices.

"You taste so fuckin' good," he said.

Tamera's response was an even louder moan. Her mouth opened and her eyes rolled up in her head. She screamed out his name as her body began to shake and tremble. Her juices cascaded out, and Rell hungrily sucked them up.

He got up on his knees and pulled out his dick. He stroked it, grinning down at her as she recovered from the orgasm. Moving forward, he slapped the head on her pussy and got ready to slide into her.

"No," she said, stopping him just before he could enter her.

She shoved him down on his back and wrapped her fingers around his heavy lovemaking pole. Her hands moved up and down, up and down, up and down, until a drop of precum oozed out of the head. Then she took him in her mouth and stuffed as much of his length in her throat as she could before her gag reflex made her yank back her head and cough. She did it again just seconds later, massaging his balls as she forced his dick to the back of her throat.

Rell relaxed and enjoyed the rapid head-bobbing that ensued. Jah did not come to his mind. Instead, he thought of what he was going to do once they left the hotel. He still had every dime of the money he'd gotten as a result of his father's untimely death. $1,184,974.86 to be exact. More money than he'd ever in his life had or even seen. Since it was Valentine's Day, and since he had just proposed to Tamera with a

$100,000 ring, he felt that it was only right to spend a little on himself and his wife-to-be.

J. Cole's Pandora station was apparently in cahoots with Drake. Two Drake songs in a row played. Rell stared up at the ceiling and listened:

"I still been drinkin' on the low, mobbin' on the low
Fuckin' on the low, smokin' on the low
I still been plottin' on the low, schemin' on the low
The furthest thing from perfect like everyone I know..."

Rell liked Drake's music. A lot of people hated on the lyrically-inclined Canadian, but not Rell. He had been rocking with Drizzy ever since he first heard the rap titan on a song with Eminem, Kanye, and Lil Wayne.

Tamera's oral skills were through the roof. She sucked tightly while stroking his length and cradling his balls. Her saliva coated his erection. She was working much harder than she usually did.

Just as Rell felt the tingle of an imminent eruption, he pushed Tamera's head up with one hand and pulled his phallus out of her mouth with the other.

"Whoa, baby. Hold on a second. Damn," he said, and chuckled once.

Tamera did not hold on for a second. She sucked his scrotum into her mouth, regarding him with a scheming smile. Her gold hoop earrings swung as wildly as her head did, and the sucking sounds coming from her mouth made it known that she was seriously trying to push him over the edge.

Rell had to literally jump out of bed to stop himself from prematurely blasting off.

Tamera sat up Indian-style and gave him an innocent look. "You alright, sweetie?" she asked, her tone replete with sarcasm.

"Fuck you, nigga," Rell replied.

"Come on, honey. It's V-Day, remember? You're supposed to be putting it down. You're supposed to be the big bad, long-dicked pussy bandit. That's how you made it seem, at least. What's the matter, grandpa didn't take his Viagra? Awww."

Rell busted out laughing as he leapt on top of Tamera. They kissed for a full minute. She had the kind of lips that a man could never get tired of kissing.

She rolled over so that she was on top, then she stood up and went to the desk. Rell watched her as she pushed the yellow chair aside, bent over the desk, and looked back at him.

"Come on, lil daddy. Show me what you got," she said.

Rell got up in a hurry and positioned himself behind her. He put his dick between her generous derrière cheeks and slid right into her slippery goodness.

She gasped reflexively.

He grabbed her shoulders and went to town, slamming in and out of her as roughly as he possibly could. Since she wanted to play games, he would give her what she was asking for. He'd fuck her so hard that afterward she would walk funny for a week.

What sounded like one long moan blew from Tamera's lips. She held on to the desk and took it like a boss chick. Rell admired her strength. He'd never fucked another girl who could take what he was giving her without quitting on him.

He lifted one of her legs up onto the desk and kept thrusting into her. He loved the way her thick butt wobbled as he pounded in and out, his left hand holding the nape of her neck in a vice-like grip.

"Say you love me," he said, in a tone of voice that was very domineering and aggressive.

When Tamera didn't reply, he pounded harder and repeated his request. This time she obliged.

"I...love... you," she said in between moans.

This is what Rell wanted. He liked this position. It put Tamera at his mercy. She had nowhere to run. Her only choice was to stand there and take it. She had asked for the same type of thug loving he'd given her that night at his mom's house, and Rell was more than happy to give it to her.

He looked down at his dick and nodded his head agreeably as he eyed the juices that coated it from tip to base. His dick was about as thick as his wrist. The girth of it stretched Tamera's vaginal walls with every savage penetration.

He fucked her this way until she had a second orgasm. Then he turned her around so that she was sitting on the desk and slid right back in, pressing his lips to hers as he did. She let out a gasp. She could not return the kiss because her mouth was wide open. She clawed at his back as he began to thrust, rocking her on the desk. She hit the back of her head on the TV as she attempted to retreat. He grabbed her hips and snatched her to him; her ass squeaked across the glass, and she let out a scream as he sank deep inside of her.

Once Tamera was able to shut her mouth, she started kissing him back as he made love to her and rubbed his hands all over her smooth chocolate skin.

Out of the corner of his eye, he saw his smartphone light up on the sofa. He was close enough to it to see that it was Jah's contact picture in the middle of the screen.

He quickly moved his attention back to Tamera. There was no need to look at the phone right now. It wasn't like he was going to stop fucking Tamera to answer it.

Tamera had tears in her eyes. Her mouth was open again. She was gasping uncontrollably, clawing at his shoulders now, lying practically limp against the wall behind her.

"You're...killing me," she said.

Rell grinned. He felt the eruption on the way. He sped up, hunched over her, and relentlessly drilled her pussy until his dick started twitching as he dumped a copious load of semen inside her.

With the last of his energy, he picked her up and carried her to the bed, kissing the tear streaks on her face. Tamera seemed too stunned to speak. She didn't utter a single word for five whole minutes.

Rell was lying next to her, smiling proudly and staring at the TV, when she swung a leg over his waist and put the side of her face on his chest.

He knew that a meaningful conversation was on the way. Every time he fucked her good she got all emotional on him. He was used to it now.

"Fuck," she said. "You're an asshole. I really cannot stand your black ass."

"What did I do this time?"

"You know exactly what the fuck you did. Jerk." He heard the tears in her voice. She was crying.

"Stop with that crybaby shit."

"If you leave me, I'm going to fucking kill you. I hope you know that. I'm so serious."

"Why would I leave you?"

"For the same reason they all leave."

"Don't compare me to no other niggas. I'm Sincere Jerrell Owens. I'm not like no other nigga in the world."

"I know that now. It's just that...I don't know. This just seems too good to be true. Like, I've never had a faithful man.

116

I keep thinking you're going to leave me like my exes did. I'd die if you went and had a baby with another bitch."

"Have a baby with another bitch? I ain't even got one baby yet. Your ass is crazy."

"I'm not crazy. I'm cautious. My heart's been broken too many times. There's a brick wall around it, and you're kicking right through it. I'm scared of that, Rell. I really am. I'm scared that you're gonna leave any day now. If you fuck another girl the same way you just fucked me, I'm going to lose you. She's not gonna want to let you go."

"Why in God's name would I put a ring on your finger and then go out and fuck somebody else? I thought the point of proposing to a woman was to let her know that you want her and only her."

Tamera paused, then, softly scraping her fingernails across his chest, she said, "Excuse my craziness." She snickered. "I can get that way sometimes. Hope you can deal with it. My granny says I get it from my momma. She says I'm the crazy one and Tirzah is the fighter."

"I knew you had some screws loose up there. It's okay. We'll get you some help. Take you to see a head doctor."

Tamera's hand moved quickly up his chest. She grabbed one nipple between her thumb and forefinger and pinched. Rell shouted, clamped a hand on her wrist, and applied pressure until she let go. He came very close to calling her a bitch.

"Asshole," she said.

"Don't do that shit no more," he warned.

"What're you gonna do?"

"Do it again and find out."

"Are we going to move off Trumbull or what? I'm sick of the hood. We need to go somewhere and find a nice-sized house to live in. We could go to Bellwood. They have nice homes for sale out there for less than a quarter million. I'll get a better job to help pay for it. What do you think?"

Rell planted a kiss on Tamera's forehead and pulled her closer. Unbeknownst to her, he was already thinking of what he was going to do with her in the immediate future.

His plans included a larger home, new cars, a business or two, and last but perhaps most important, a baby.

Chapter 20

Instead of getting out of the car and giving it up to the robbers, Zo had stomped down on the gas pedal and ducked his head, swerving right and crashing through the high school's rear fence. He'd felt the bullets whizzing by his head. He'd heard them pinging through the big white Chevy's steel exterior. But he'd kept his head — and ultimately his life — by veering onto Millard and racing away from the robbers.

When he made it to his sister Odella's house on Spaulding in the bullet-riddled car, she had been standing on the porch with a few of their cousins, all of them grieving over Roddy's murder and talking about how bad the gun violence was getting in their neighborhood. Neither of them had noticed all the bullet holes in his car.

Instead of going into his sister's house, he had crossed the street and knocked on Zaniyah's door. She let him in and he saw that she'd been sitting in the living room with her friend Lisa, drinking Hennessy and smoking cigarettes.

Zo sat down on Zaniyah's threadbare brown sofa and shut his eyes for a long time. Tears fell, but he said not a single word. Zaniyah and Lisa offered their condolences, but they fell on deaf ears. Zo was suffering from post-traumatic stress. All the gunshots and deaths he'd experienced over the past few months had taken a toll on his sixteen-year-old brain. He wondered if someone would walk in the door and shoot him square in the head while his eyes were shut but he did not open them. With Roddy gone, he didn't really care anymore. He just wanted to avenge his brother's death before it was all said and done. He wanted to blow Jah's brains out the same way Jah had blown Roddy's brains out. After that, he didn't care what happened.

"I was standing right there next to him when it happened," Zaniyah was saying. "He made me call Roddy over there. He had a gun on me. I couldn't do nothing but do what he told me to do. I was so scared. You know Tangie was my cousin, and look at what happened to her. Somebody shot her in the head. Shot her sister in the head, too. I'm terrified of that happening to me. When Jah pulled that gun on me, I just about pissed my pants, and when he shot Roddy, I just took off running. I didn't know what else to do."

"I would've done the same thing, girl," Lisa said. "Ain't nothing wrong with running when a nigga got a gun. All that brave shit ain't about nothing. Better save yourself."

"Yeah, but I feel so bad. I was just telling Jah how much I liked you, Zo. I swear on my momma I was. I had just told him, and he reached in his Pelle and upped the gun on me. He made me walk to the alley, to the back of the dope line. He made me shout for Roddy. After that shit happened, I started to go over there to his house on Trumbull and burn that bitch to the ground. Everybody knows he got the upstairs apartment and Rell got the one on the first floor. Hell, if the police hadn't pulled up so deep, I probably would have done it. Lord knows he deserves it for taking that poor lil boy's life. Nobody that young deserves to be shot down like that."

It was Zaniyah's mention of Jah's house on Trumbull that made Zo open his eyes. He looked at Zaniyah.

"You think he's at that house? The house on Trumbull. Think he's there now?"

She shrugged. "I'd guess not. I don't think he's going to stay right here in the hood knowing that I saw him shoot Roddy. He don't know if I told the police or what."

"Did you?"

"Hell no! I ain't no snitch. I don't talk to no fucking cops. You know me better than that, Zo. I told you and Lisa. That's all the telling I'ma do."

Zo nodded his head slowly and stood up. He went to the living room window and looked out. There were four Chicago Police Department vehicles at the corner, and one officer had just walked over to Zo's car. He seemed to be investigating the bullet holes.

Zaniyah asked Zo about the blood on his hands and clothes but he ignored her and headed for the back door. He left and jogged down the stairs and into the alley, which he took all the way to Douglas Boulevard before he turned left and made his way toward Trumbull Avenue.

Chapter 21

"Just lay here and relax for a few hours. Don't nobody know where I live anyway. Unless you told that nigga," Jah said as he tucked Felicia under the covers in his bed.

"I would never tell a nigga where you live, or anything else about you. You're my daughter's father. I'd never betray you."

"I hope not."

"Come on, now, Jahlil. You should know that. Have I ever done some snake shit to you? Knowingly, I mean. You know that I would never have even fucked with that boy had I known what was going on."

Jah grinned. He gave Felicia a kiss on the tip of her nose and then picked up Dora's car seat from the foot of the bed. Dora was already back to her usual happy demeanor, smiling up at Jah with one hand balled into a fist and stuffed halfway in her mouth.

"Don't tell my momma about Zo hurting me," Felicia said, holding the towel-wrapped bag of ice to her head. "She'll throw a whole damn fit about it. Just tell her that we need her to watch Dora for a day or two while we get some things figured out."

Jah nodded. "I got'chu, baby. No worries. Get some rest. I'll be right back."

For some reason Felicia found interest in the Chicago skyline on the back of Jah's leather Pelle Pelle jacket as he left the bedroom. She thought it might be because she'd known Jah since he was twelve years old and had never seen him looking so fresh. He was becoming a man, and she found it sexy.

She breathed a sigh of relief when she heard him leave out the back door.

"Fuck my life," she muttered vacantly as she grabbed the television remote control and turned to Fox News.

As always, the news was about the endless shootings throughout the city's Black and Hispanic neighborhoods. People were calling for the National Guard. The CPD lieutenant was calling for stricter penalties against gang members who were caught with firearms. Father Pfleger was upset about an eleven-year-old girl who was shot and killed last night in Englewood.

There was also breaking news of Roddy's murder on 15th and Spaulding.

Felicia sighed and shook her head. She rubbed her belly and wondered if she should get an abortion. After all that had gone down today, she knew that she wanted nothing more to do with Zo, and she didn't want to be tied to him by the birth of what would be her second child.

She pushed a hand down in her purse and fished out her smartphone. She dialed her sister Candace's number and put the phone to her ear, lowering the TV volume with the remote.

"What's up, sis?" Candace answered in her deep voice. She was a masculine lesbian who loved to play basketball and watch sports. Sometimes Felicia believed that God had actually meant to make Candace a boy, but had accidentally given her female genitalia.

"I'm ready to kill that nigga Zo," Felicia said. "He pistol-whipped me. In front of Dora, too. Got my face all busted up and swollen. Ugh, I could kill that nigga. Literally."

Candace took a few seconds to take it all in before she replied, "You got your gun?"

"Nope, my dumb ass left it in the closet. I got Jah's gun under the pillow I'm laying on right now, though. Let his ass come at me again and I'm knocking holes in his bitch ass."

"Where's Dora?"

"Jah's taking her home to Momma. He should be walking through the door any minute now."

"Bitch...why the fuck did Zo beat on you?"

"Because Roddy got killed and he thinks Jah did it. He wanted to get back at Jah, I guess. Girl, I was so damn scared. I can't even lie. He went crazy on me out the blue. I was coming to him to complain about the fight I had just had with Jah, not knowing that his brother had just got killed. It's too crazy."

"You at Jah's house on Trumbull?"

Just as Felicia was getting ready to answer the question, she heard the doorbell ring.

"Was that the doorbell?" Candace asked.

"Yeah." Felicia sat up. "Yeah, I'm at Jah's house, and yeah, that was the doorbell."

The doorbell rang again.

"Take that gun with you if you're gonna answer that door," Candace said.

"Girl, I hope it is that nigga. I'ma blast his punk ass right in the face."

"Don't hang up. I wanna listen. And I'm on my way over there."

Felicia slipped her hand under the pillow and curled her fingers around the handle of Jah's .45-caliber handgun before pushing the blanket and sheet down and swinging her legs over the side of the bed.

The doorbell rang twice more.

"It's probably just Jah's momma," Felicia said, speaking more to herself than to her sister.

"Don't just open the door. Ask who it is first," Candace advised.

"Duh, bitch. You think I'm that damn stupid? Fuck I look like, one of those dumb white bitches in a scary movie?"

"I'm just saying."

Felicia stepped into her sneakers and walked out into the hallway. She paused, listening, then continued on to the living room door.

She opened it and peered down the stairs at the door that led out to the front porch. There were three triangular windows at the top of the door. She could not see anyone through them.

"Who is it?" Candace asked.

"Hell, I don't fucking know. Let me get to the damn door first," Felicia whispered back.

She started down the stairs with the gun at her side, moving timidly, afraid that Zo might be standing on the other side of the door and forcing herself to be ready to shoot if that was the case.

She made it to the door and took a deep breath to settle her rattled mind. Then she took another deep breath, and another.

The doorbell chimed yet again.

"Who is it?" Felicia said.

A barrage of gunshots followed.

Felicia gasped as bullet after bullet pierced the door. She felt them burning through her legs, and her stomach, and her chest. The next thing she knew she was on the floor at the foot of the staircase, struggling to breathe, reaching for her phone, which was just out of reach.

The last thing she heard was her sister's panicked screams.

Chapter 22

"You alright in there, sweetheart? Come on out so we can talk. We ain't gotta have no sex. I understand. Talk to me."

Tirzah was sitting on the bathroom floor with her back against the door, her knees pulled up to her chest, and her face pressed down on her crossed arms. She was crying. She didn't want to talk to Tremaine. The only person she wanted to hear right now was Jahlil Owens.

An empty bottle of champagne lay on the floor next to her. She had drank it all by herself, which was part of the reason she was feeling all emotional about losing Jah.

"I don't want to talk, Tremaine. Just...give me a minute. I'll be out in one minute, okay?"

She heard his footfalls as he walked away from the door. Raising her head, she sniffled and thumbed the tears off her face. She picked up her iPhone and went to her photo gallery.

She had hundreds of pictures of herself with Jah, so many that she wondered if she had been a little too heavy with the picture-snapping. Maybe that was why Jah had broken up with her. Maybe she was showing too much affection, suffocating him with too much attention. She knew that Jah was a street nigga to the core. He was the type that didn't like a lot of attention.

"Why am I sitting here crying over a fucking teenager when I'm four years away from thirty?" she asked herself, shaking her head as she stood up and studied herself in the sink mirror.

She sighed and shut off her phone screen. There was no sense in crying over someone who didn't want her when she had a perfectly good man waiting on her not even twenty feet away.

She shook her head. She was buzzing good off the champagne. She fixed her makeup and left the bathroom wearing a forced smile.

Tremaine had a football game playing on the TV. He was on the sofa, drinking from a glass of iced cognac. He was a lot taller than Jah. He had gray stubble on his chin and more than a few more grays on his head.

The way he ogled Tirzah reminded her of how a pedophile might look at a playground full of children. It kind of creeped her out.

"You alright?" He put his glass on the ottoman and sat forward. His hungry eyes ascended from her heels to her breasts and finally to her face. He licked his lips and rubbed the knees of his slacks. "You seem bothered. Sounded like I heard you crying in there."

"No, I'm fine." Tirzah sat down on the bed and stared at her iPhone's screen, silently wishing that Jah would just call and apologize and beg her for forgiveness. He wouldn't have to do much begging. She was ready to jump in his lap at this point.

Jah must have read her mind, because at that very moment her smartphone rang and his contact photo popped up.

Tirzah's eyes grew wide. She hopped up and ran back into the bathroom, answering the call as she went.

"Hello?" she said.

"The fuck you doin'?" Jah replied.

Tirzah smiled as she shut and locked the door. "Nothing. Why?"

Jah paused. Tirzah's smile broadened. Tears filled her eyes again, only now they were tears of joy.

"I'm sorry," Jah said. "I shouldn't have said that dumb shit this morning. I was dumb. I'm apologizing for the shit."

"Well, I forgive you."

"The fuck is up with that date, though? You on a date on Valentine's Day and it ain't me? Fuck kinda shit is that?"

"Don't play me, Jah. This is your fault. I would've never even come here with this lame ass nigga if you hadn't ditched me like that."

"Who is he?"

"Tremaine. An older guy who's been trying to get at me since I was your age. I only did it to make you jealous." She smiled at herself in the mirror. "Sounds like it worked."

"Tirzah, don't make me fuck you up and make that nigga watch you take that ass-whippin' before I beat his ass just like I did yours. Play with me if you want to."

"Mm. I like it when you get jealous like this." She laughed. "Where are you? Where's your girlfriend?"

"That bitch ain't my girlfriend."

"Well, your baby momma."

"That nigga Zo pistol-whipped her. I let her lay in my bed at the house. Was just about to drop my baby off but now I'm coming to get you. Where you at? And if you fucked that old-ass nigga I'm fucking you up."

"I didn't fuck that lame-ass old man. I'm at the W Hotel, on Lake Shore Drive. Third floor. Room 314."

"Stay there. I'm on my way."

Tirzah was just about to tell him not to hang up but it was too late. He had already ended the call. She sighed, dropped her head in defeat, and opened the door...only to find herself standing face to face with Tremaine.

She was raising her head to look up at him when he clamped his hands around her throat and violently threw her to the back of the bathroom. She hit the rear wall hard and slid down to the floor. She was trying to get up when he kneed her in the face and punched her in the jaw.

"Lame-ass old man? I'm a lame-ass old man to you?!"
He punched her several more times in the head. "Bitch, I'll
show you a lame. Give you some of this lame dick. Lay down,
hoe. Lay down before I catch a murder case up in this mutha-
fucka."

Tirzah tried once more to get up. Tremaine grabbed her
head and slammed her face on the floor. Then he rammed her
head into the side of the tub again and again until, crying out
in pain, she said, "Okay, okay. Alright. Just stop hurting me."

He shoved her down on her stomach and pushed up her
dress. She closed her eyes and felt wetness under her face.

She was bleeding.

He didn't care. He put his mouth right up against her left
ear.

"You wanna play me like some goddamn simp! Huh,
bitch? Is that what you think of me? You think I'm just some
kind of hoe-ass nigga? Bitch, you wish you had a nigga like
me. You ain't never seen a nigga like me. I'm the realest nigga
you'll ever meet, but since you wanna play me like I'm some
hoe ass nigga I'ma show you. I'ma show you right goddamn
now."

He entered her roughly, and the first thing that came to
her mind was that he might have an STD. She hoped he was
clean.

She also hoped that Jah would not take long to make it
here to room 314.

Chapter 23

The Escalade rode so smoothly that Jah reclined in his seat and drove like he was the coolest seventeen-year-old in all of Chicago. Or Chiraq, as he preferred to call it.

He was upset that he didn't have his smartphone charger. His iPhone had died on him a few minutes prior, just as Felicia's sister, Candace, had been calling him. He figured it was just Candace calling to see where he was, since he should have arrived at her mother's house to drop off Dora by now.

He stopped at a red light and looked back at Dora. She was fast asleep in her car seat, her pacifier hanging out the side of her mouth, the foot of a small pink teddy bear held loosely in her left hand. She looked a lot like Jah in the face. Every time he looked at her, his heart swelled with love. She was his sweet little angel. Daddy's little girl. He could not remember ever being happier than he'd been the day Dora was born. He loved her more than he loved himself. Her birth had given him hope. He couldn't wait for her to start talking. He hoped that her first word would be "Da-Da".

He found something smooth on the radio to listen to — a Jennifer Hudson song about love — and drove off down Lake Shore Drive with a smile on his face.

His mind went to wondering if Tirzah was telling the truth about not having fucked the old guy. He hoped she hadn't. He didn't think he would be able to forgive her if she had. In the past, he had messed around with some girls who'd fucked just about everyone in the neighborhood and he had not cared one bit, but things were different with Tirzah. She had his heart. He couldn't remember ever loving a girl the way he loved her.

Rell had told him earlier about the idea to propose to Tamera.

Maybe that's what Jah needed to do.

He detoured and drove over to Michigan Avenue. The biggest smile crossed his face as he pulled up to Tiffany and Co. He took the American Express card out of his wallet and inhaled sharply. Finally, he was about to spend some of the money he'd inherited from his father.

Chapter 24

The idea came to Kendrick out of nowhere.

He was mingling with his family at the "Welcome Home" party his mother had set up for him at her home on 15th and Christiana when he thought of it.

During the celebration, he learned from several of his cousins that Jah had just killed Zo's younger brother. It had happened just one block away on Spaulding.

His cousin Darryl gave him $400, a True Religion outfit, and a pair of Air Force One sneakers. After getting dressed and eating his fill of the delicious food his mother had cooked for him, he got the keys to her old-school Lincoln Continental and drove around the corner to look at the crime scene for himself. Then he dialed a number on the smartphone Lashaunda had given him as he drove off.

"Detective Givens?" he said as soon as the call was answered.

"Yeah, who's this?"

"Kendrick. Kendrick Robertson."

The detective chuckled once. "You got something for me already? Christ, that was quick. You've hardly been out an hour."

"I don't exactly have it yet. Just want to get a few things clear." Kendrick pulled to a stop at the convenience store on the corner of 16th and Drake. He waved and smiled at a group of teenage girls as they walked out of the store.

"What is it?"

"Well," Kendrick said, lighting a cigarette, "I think I can do something better than just giving you a dope boy. If you can get all those charges expunged from my record, end my parole, and promise to keep me in the clear for at least the next couple of months, I can give you one of the real shooters. I mean the man who's responsible for most of the murders in North Lawndale. The same guy who just killed the boy on 15th and Spaulding."

"Come on, Robertson. You can't be serious. I just got you out of prison, and all we got out of that was one measly drug conviction. To give you that much leeway, this guy has to be a bigger threat to the city than those Lamron Black Disciples."

"He is."

"Yeah? Give me the names of some of his victims."

Kendrick grinned and eased back in the driver's seat, knowing that he had exactly what the detective needed. He had learned enough from Zo to make Detective Givens give him everything he wanted.

"Remember the guy who was killed in the alley behind the house on 13th and Avers? Jamie? And Stain, the one who was found dead in the car on Independence? And the two guys who got smoked on Albany, right off Douglas? When the little girl got killed in the crossfire? Oh, and Martez, who got whacked at the building on Homan? Or what about the two girls who were killed behind the house on 16th and St. Louis? Yeah, all of them are connected, and I know everything."

The detective took a moment to respond. Kendrick blew rings of smoke at the roof and combed out his beard while he waited.

"The biggest thing you've got is the little girl's murder. There's a fifty-thousand-dollar reward for an arrest in that case."

"I want that, too. I need that fifty grand."

"Who is he?"

"No. It won't be that easy."

"Don't bullshit with me, Robertson. I'll have your ass back in Stateville so fast your head will spin. Give me a name."

"I want all my demands signed off on before I do any name-giving. I've been lied to way too many times to play the fool on this one. Make the necessary calls. I know that if anybody can make it happen it's you. I want this damn leash cut from around my neck. Let me breathe and I'll give you what you want."

Detective Givens sighed. "Let me call the DA's office. I'll hit you right back."

"I'll be waiting."

"I need the name of that little girl's killer."

"And I need to be free from going back to prison. Favor for a favor."

Kendrick ended the call feeling happier than he'd felt beforehand. He got out of the car and went in the store to buy a pack of cigarettes and some potato chips. While waiting behind a pregnant woman at the counter, he overheard her tell her friend that Jah's baby's momma had just gotten "hit up" at Jah's house on Trumbull. Knowing that this was the perfect time to make his move, Kendrick pulled out his phone and dialed Tamera's number.

Chapter 25

She was sleeping soundly on Rell's chest, dreaming about a beautiful wedding that included her father in the ceremony, only instead of the dope fiend her father was in real life, he was dressed fresh and clean cut as he walked her down the aisle.

Her wedding dress was snow-white and as bright as the sunlight that somehow spilled through the roof above. All of her family was present on one side of the aisle, along with two girls she hadn't liked in high school, an old neighbor, and a guy she'd worked at Dunkin Donuts with.

She awoke to the sound of her phone ringing and immediately woke Rell up to tell him about the dream as she went to the desk and reached in her purse for her phone.

"I just had the craziest dream," she said.

"You couldn't wait to let me know that?"

"I didn't want to forget the damn dream," she explained as she looked at her phone. "I bet this is that nigga Kendrick again. I don't know this number."

Rell got up and walked to her, twisting the palms of his hands on his eyes. He took the phone, looked at it, and then answered the call, putting it on speakerphone so that Tamera could also hear.

"Hello?"

"Who is this, Rell?" It was definitely Kendrick.

"Man, how many times—"

"I ain't tryna hear that shit, nigga. I need fifty racks or your brother is over with. I know about all the bodies he done dropped. I know he just whacked Lil Roddy. I'll give his ass right up, nigga. Think I'm playing if you wanna. I just got off the line with the chief of homicide, nigga. I want that money right now. And you better hurry up before he calls me back."

Rell regarded Tamera with a look of sheer disbelief. He mouthed, "Is this nigga serious?"

Tamera said, "Are you fucking serious, Kendrick? So, you're a snitch now?"

"Hey, you can call it whatever you wanna call it. Just run me that money. I tried to be nice and just ask for the shit. Y'all made me take it this far. I spent about fifty bands on you and Tirzah, and I want my shit back."

"Fifty bands? Is that code for five hundred dollars? Because I know damn well you don't mean fifty thousand dollars. You can get all that cheap-ass furniture back whenever you want it. And that broke down-ass car. We don't need any of it."

"I'm sure you don't. Look, I don't got time for all this chit chat. Y'all gon' give me the money or what? Hurry up and let me know so I can know what I'ma tell this detective when he calls back."

Tamera looked at Rell. His face was tight. His free hand was balled into a fist. His eyes were cold and full of anger.

"Is that a yes or a no?" Kendrick asked.

Rell said, "We ain't got that much money. The most I can come up with is thirty-five. That's all we got. You can take it or leave it. Thirty-five thousand in cash. I can hit you with it by midnight. After that. I don't wanna hear from you again. Deal?"

Kendrick took a moment to reply. By then, Rell had taken a half dozen deep breaths, balling and unballing his left hand while typing on his smartphone with his other one.

"I'll take that for now, but I need that other fifteen by the end of the month. I don't give a fuck if you gotta sell that building on Homan to get it. I'm turning over the info I got on Jah to the law if you don't pay up. I hope you don't think I'm bullshitting."

"I'll get you the other fifteen by then. Chill out on that police-ass shit, nigga. I said I got'chu. Just make sure that you don't go talking to no cops. I don't do that rat shit, nigga. Fuck kinda niggas raised you?"

"Don't worry about who raised me. Just worry about getting that money together. I'll call back in two hours for a drop spot. If you ain't got it by then, that's your brother's ass."

Kendrick was laughing as he ended the call, leaving Tamera standing there fuming. She put down her smartphone and gazed at Rell as he began pacing a tight circle at the foot of the bed and typing on his own smartphone.

"Well," Tamera said, shaking her head, "I guess this isn't the best time to tell you about the dream I just had."

Rell didn't even look her way.

With a despondent sigh, she sat down and tried to think of a way to keep Jah out of jail if Kendrick ended up snitching. First and foremost, Jah would definitely have to get rid of every gun he ever used to kill someone. That was a must. Secondly, he'd have to make sure that there was no other evidence that could be used against him.

"Jah is a pain in your side, isn't he?" Tamera said. She looked over at Rell. He was getting dressed and texting on his phone at the same time. His expression was just as furious as it had been seconds prior.

Just then, Tamera got a text from Sarah, a girl who lived across the street from them on Trumbull:

"Tam please tell me ur ok paramedics just carried a body out of ur house the front door is all shot up. What's going on over there girl call me when u get this text"

Tamera's mouth fell open. She turned to Rell, who was already looking at her.

"I know," he said. "Just was texting Candace. It's Felicia. She say Zo had pistol-whipped Felicia and that Jah had let her in the house to lay down. Candace was on the phone with Felicia when somebody pressed the doorbell. Candace stayed on the phone with Felicia while she went to answer the door. Then she heard gunshots."

"You think it was Zo?"

"Well, I mean, I doubt if it was your police-ass boyfriend."

Tamera squinted at Rell. He quickly reworded the accusation.

"You know what I mean. Your ex-boyfriend. Ex-cop friend. Whatever the fuck he is. Rat-ass nigga. He better hope I don't see him nowhere in the hood. I'ma—"

"You're not going to do anything, Rell. I absolutely refuse to let that fool ruin what we have going. I'm getting my wedding. Hell, J-Lo was at my damn wedding."

Rell frowned. "J-Lo? You smoke something while I was asleep?"

"If you had listened to the dream, you would know what I'm talking about. But whatever. Bottom line is, I'm not letting him fuck this up. There's a way around this. We just have to think."

"I tried calling Jah. The nigga got his phone turned off."

Tamera was getting dressed. She sent Tirzah a text and told her to come over to hers and Rell's suite for an important talk. Then she sent a text to Tara saying the same thing. She had a flawless white diamond on her finger that was bigger than any diamond she'd ever seen up close, and she was determined to marry the man who'd given it to her.

Nothing was going to get in the way of her marriage.

Chapter 26

The elevator door slid open and Jah smiled at the tall stranger who was standing there waiting to get on the elevator. The man was tall and slim, and he seemed to be in a hurry. Jah was holding Dora's car seat in one hand and her diaper bag in the other. He was excited about the ring he'd just bought for Tirzah. It wasn't as large as the one his brother had just proposed to Tamera with, but it was nice nonetheless, a five-carat cushion cut white diamond ring that had cost him $12,000.

He could not wait to get down on one knee and put it on Tirzah's finger.

The skinny man didn't speak. Jah thought he remembered seeing the man at a restaurant on the west side not too long ago, but he wasn't sure. It was only when he had stepped out of the elevator and headed up the black-carpeted hallway that he considered the fact that the skinny man might have been the older guy who was Tirzah's date. By then, the elevator door had closed.

Tara and K emerged from a room further down the hall just as Jah made it to room 314.

Tara's eyes got big.

"I don't think you should go in there," she said. "How'd you even know where to find her?"

"She told me." Jah set the diaper bag down and knocked on the door.

Then he saw Tamera's head peek out of a door toward the end of the hallway.

Tamera gasped. "Come down here, Jah," she said quickly. Then she looked at Tara. "Who in the hell told him to go to that room?"

Jah laughed. He knew what they were so worried about. They thought that Tirzah might be in the room having sex with her date.

"It's cool." Jah chuckled and shook his head. "She told me what room she was in. She ain't fuckin' with dude."

He knocked on the door again.

Rell walked out of the room down the hall with Tamera trailing closely behind him.

"Tirzah!" Jah shouted, still knocking. "It's me, baby. Open the door."

When Rell was just a couple of feet away from Jah, he said, "You heard about what happened to Felicia?"

Jah looked at his big brother and nodded his head yes. "I'm the one who picked her up after the shit happened. Hoe-ass nigga pistol-whipped her. I put her in bed and told her to get some rest. She's at the house."

"No, I mean the shooting at the house."

Jah became thoughtful. A shooting? What shooting was Rell referring to?

"Somebody rang the doorbell and when she went to answer it, they shot her up," Rell said. "Ambulance just rushed her to the hospital."

The news hit Jah like a cannonball to the chest. He put down the car seat and stared at Rell, hoping that this was some kind of sick joke, but somehow knowing that it wasn't. Suddenly, he could feel his heart beating. Boom-boom, boom-boom, boom-boom. He could feel his teeth grinding together. He felt like he was observing himself from the outside. Felicia had been the love of his life since way back in the day. He simply could not picture her being dead and gone.

Dora started crying, as if she understood what was being said about her mother. Rell rushed over and scooped her out of the car seat. Tamera was at Jah's side just seconds later, knocking on Tirzah's hotel room door.

Jah was so stunned by the news of Felicia being shot that he stood there and said nothing for a moment. He heard Rell telling him something about Kendrick trying to snitch on him but it went in one ear and out the other.

He didn't snap out of the daze until he heard Tirzah scream for help.

Chapter 27

As soon as Tirzah was able to move the towel Tremaine had tied around her mouth, she screamed, "Help! Somebody come and untie me! I've been raped! Help!"

She had heard Jah knocking on the door and telling her to open it for him, and she was elated to see him kick the door open.

She was hogtied on the bed, her ankles and wrists bound together with a bed sheet. Tamera freed her from the restraints while Jah searched through the room with his gun in hand.

"It's no use," Tirzah said sobbingly. "He just left. He overheard me talking to you on the phone and got mad because I called him a lame. The bitch nigga raped me."

Tamera wrapped a blanket around Tirzah's naked body, and for a while, Tirzah rocked back and forth and just cried. Never in her life had she felt so violated. She hated all the killing that had been going on lately, but now she wanted to kill Tremaine, and she didn't care if she went to prison for the rest of her life for doing it, either.

She was able to calm down when Rell placed Dora in her arms. Dora stopped crying immediately and reached a hand up to grab Tirzah's bottom lip. Jah sat down next to her and wrapped his arms around her.

"Don't even trip, baby. On my life, I'm about to go and find that nigga. I think he just walked right past me, too. I know how he look. I'm on his ass, baby. On King Neal, I'm on that nigga as soon as I catch him."

She looked over at Jah and was surprised to see that he, too, had tears in his eyes. She had previously thought that she'd never live to see the day when Jah would shed another tear after his father's funeral.

He kissed her on the cheek and hugged her tighter against him.

She told him what Tremaine had been wearing when he left and Jah confirmed that he had indeed crossed paths with Tremaine while stepping out of the elevator.

He got up to go and try to find Tremaine, but Tirzah stopped him.

"Let him go," she said. "I know exactly where to find him."

Tamera nodded her head. "Yup. We found his ass earlier, and we'll find him there again. It's his family's business. I bet he shows his face there before the day is over."

"And when he does," Tirzah said, wiping away her tears and studying Dora's pretty little face, "I'm going to shoot him myself. He raped the wrong bitch."

Chapter 28

The ride back to the west side of the city was for the most part silent. Jah sat in the backseat between Dora's car seat and Tirzah, who laid her head in his lap just like she'd done the night he and Rell had rescued her from the trunk of Zo's box Chevy. He rubbed her shoulder and kissed her on the ear and told her that everything was going to be okay. He thought about all the bad things that were happening and blamed himself for the majority of it. If he hadn't broken up with Tirzah this morning, none of this would have gone down. It hurt him even more knowing that it was partially his fault that she'd been raped. Rell was right: Jah had a lot of growing up to do, and he vowed that today would be the beginning of that growth.

He looked over at Dora and put his hand on her stomach so that she could grab on his fingers the way she always did. Her eyes got wide as soon as she saw his hand, and she laughed as she curled her fingers around his thumbs.

"I love you, little lady," he said to Dora. "Daddy loves you. Daddy will always love you. I hope you know that."

What happened next shocked him.

"Da...Da." Dora smiled.

Jah's eyes lit up and his heart swelled with joy. He looked to the front passenger seat and saw that Rell was looking back and smiling at him.

"Bruh, you heard that shit?" Jah asked.

Rell nodded. "I heard it."

"She said Da-Da." Jah got excited. He gave his baby girl a kiss. She slobbered on his lower lip, grabbed his nose, and said "Da" again as he lifted his head.

He had Rell check his phone, which was plugged up to Tamera's charger. It was at thirty-one percent. He turned it on and dialed Candace's number.

"Shit, Jah. What the fuck, man? I've been calling you like crazy. Somebody shot Felicia. I'm pretty sure it was Zo."

"I know. Rell told me what happened. Is she alright?"

"We're at the hospital. It doesn't look good. She was hit five times. Twice in the chest, once in the stomach, and two times in her legs. She's in surgery now."

"Anybody know where Zo went?"

"If we did, he'd be just as shot up as my sister. Ol' bitch-ass nigga. Gon' shoot a girl. I can't believe this shit. If my sister dies..."

Candace tried to keep going, but she broke down and started crying. Her sister's hospitalization was too much to bear. Jah understood her pain. He, too, was hurt. He loved Felicia. He might not have been in love with her — he was in love with Tirzah Lyon — but he definitely loved her.

He hung up and put the phone down. His mind wandered a mile a minute. He wanted to find Zo and kill him for shooting Felicia. He wanted to find Tremaine and kill him for raping Tirzah. He wanted to find Kendrick and kill him for threatening to snitch. There just wasn't enough time in the day to handle all of his wants.

"We gotta get these niggas handled, big bruh. Not tomorrow, not next week. Today," Jah said to Rell. "I'm tryna be all good and shit and these niggas just keep trying my patience. Well, I'm done being good. They want the bad guy, I'ma give it to 'em."

Tamera looked over at Rell and then glanced back at Jah. "Good guy? Either my definition of good is wrong, or he means Good Guy like the Chucky doll."

"Fuck all that," Jah said to Rell. "What's up? What we on? You know what I wanna do to all three of 'em."

Rell nodded his head. "You already know what it is. Let's catch up with Momma and get her situated first. Shit, we might not even have to deal with the nigga Kendrick. I sent out a few text messages to the guys. Put ten on his head. You know he ain't gon' last no time in the hood with ten racks on his head. Niggas out there ready to kill for twenty-five hundred. I really ain't trying to get too involved in none of this shit myself. I just proposed to my baby, and I don't wanna be blowing kisses at her through that thick-ass glass at the county jail."

"Fuck all that." This was one of Jah's most commonly used phrases. "Just drop me off on 13th with the guys. Tell Momma she ain't gotta go nowhere. We got Johnny B, Lil Larry, Oso, Slick, Tiny, King — we don't need nobody else to handle our business. All of our lil niggas out there with choppas. We can have 'em slide on Kendrick, Zo, and that hoe ass nigga Tremaine. Whatever the case, I ain't about to just chill out while all these pussies breathing. I want 'em all dead before I go to sleep tonight."

Rell only nodded and turned the music up. Twista and the Speedknot Mobstaz's "Warm Embrace" began throbbing from the speakers in back.

The trip to the jewelry store on the Magnificent Mile resurfaced in Jah's mind. He had the ring in the front left pocket of his jeans. Although he wasn't normally the loving type, he knew deep down that Tirzah was the one. Maybe the ring was what she needed to brighten her day - a day that he had made gloomy from the time they woke up this morning. He felt that it was his responsibility to brighten it for her. He hoped that the ring would do the trick.

Chapter 29

The tears were flowing. The liquor was flowing. The house was so thick with Kush smoke that it was difficult to see more than a few feet in either direction.

Most of the people in Odella's house were family members. Some were just friends and neighbors who had known Roddy and were there to give their condolences.

Zo had tears rolling down his face. He'd lost his best friend today. He was sitting next to the sofa in a chair that he'd dragged out of the kitchen because there had been no seats left on either of the sofas. The blunt of Kush he had pinched between his thumb and forefinger was personal. He was smoking it to the face while he reminisced about all the good times he'd spent with his little brother.

He was on his second cup of Hennessy. Zaniyah was standing behind his chair with her hands on his shoulders and her chin propped up on the top of his head. The music — a Sicko Mobb track — was blasting from Odella's bedroom. There were over a dozen young Vice Lords who worked for Zo standing and sitting around the living room and walking through the house. Zo had spent over $2,500 on catered food, liquor, and Kush for everyone.

He had no appetite, and he doubted if his appetite would be coming back anytime soon.

Zaniyah moved her chin to his left shoulder and said, "That girl on Trumbull. Felicia. You did that, didn't you?"

He didn't reply.

"Well, I know you did it. This shit is getting so wild, man. I know you must be tore up inside. First you lost E and Lil Chris. Now Roddy, your own blood. It probably feels like shit can't possibly get any worse, but you gotta keep the faith, baby boy. You have to. Don't let these niggas win. You know

151

where to find Jah and Rell. I suggest you get them before they can get you. Especially Jah. I wouldn't worry too much about Rell. He ain't really in the streets like he used to be. It's Jah who's the problem. That nigga is just too damn dangerous. Something has to be done about him. If I could, I'd do it my-self. That nigga put that gun to my stomach. That's basically threatening my life. I told my brothers. They played hard at first and then turned it on me and said I shouldn't have been over there in the first place. Ol' scary asses. They're just scared of Jah like everybody else around here."

Zo turned up his Styrofoam cup and drank some of the iced cognac. It played like a flamethrower in his throat. He was listening to Zaniyah, but he was in no mood to talk. His mind was on one thing and one thing only, and that was re-venge.

His mother, Patricia, walked in a couple of minutes later, looking a hot mess. Her hair was in disarray, her coat was stained and full of holes, her jeans looked like they had not been washed in months, and she had lost about thirty pounds and four more teeth since Zo had last seen her. She was a ter-ribly thin woman. Her complexion was a shade darker than Zo's. Her heroin addiction had been bad, and now she'd grad-uated to meth, which explained her loss of teeth. She had her head down, doing her best to make it seem like she was dis-traught over Roddy's murder, but Zo knew that it was only a part of her scheme. As soon as she spotted him in the living room, she rushed over and hugged him.

"These streets will chew you up and spit you right back out, ain't that what I always told ya? Look at what done hap-pened to ya brotha. Just look at it. It's a damn shame. Niggas out here don't care 'bout a damn thing no more. I done spent my last damn forty dollars to get over here. I was way out south. Had to take four buses and the last one broke down, so I had to get a damn cab."

There was the scheme. She was going to ask him for at least forty dollars. He stared at her with an indecipherable expression on his face. He was just as disgusted by the sight of Patricia as he'd always been. Usually he chastised her for not caring enough for her kids to leave the drugs alone, but things were different now. Now he was one of the biggest dope boys in the neighborhood. He had more respect for the dope game than he had before, because now that he was making the money, he knew that drug addicts were a part of the game.

He didn't even bother arguing with Patricia about her lies. He dug in his pocket for his rubber-banded knot of cash and gave her a fifty-dollar bill.

Her eyes lit up when she saw him thumbing through the huge fold of cash. She looked him up and down, as if she was just now seeing that he was no longer the broke and poorly dressed kid he'd been the last time they saw each other.

"Boy, what you done did, robbed a bank or somethin'? Where in the hell you get all this money from? You know I'm living in a damn alley out south? Next to a garbage can that we set fires in to stay warm? And you sitting here with all this damn money? I need a lot more than fifty measly-ass dollars."

Zo looked up at Patricia. His expression did not change. He didn't want to talk but he knew that something must be said, so he gave her a piece of his mind.

"You made your own bed. Lay in it. Don't blame me for it. You gave up on me and Roddy to be a dope fiend. It ain't my business how or where you live. Now, get out my face and be happy for that fifty, 'cause right about now I feel like fucking somebody up, and it would be a shame for me to take it out on my momma."

He got up and told Zaniyah to follow him. He'd had enough of watching everyone celebrate on his dime. He needed some fresh air and privacy, just him and Zaniyah and the darkening Chicago skyline.

Patricia followed him outside.

He looked back at her and gritted his teeth together, but he kept walking. She stopped on the bottom stair of the front porch and put her hands on her hips, scowling indignantly, puffing on a cigarette she'd just taken from behind her ear and lit as they left.

Zo was just about to get in his Chevy when he looked up the street and saw a police car parked with its hood facing him. He remembered seeing the cop investigating the bullet holes in his Chevy and decided against driving it.

Lucky for him, he had purchased a jet black, four-year-old Cadillac CTS just last week for $14,000. He'd only driven it twice. This would be his third drive.

He got in the driver's seat and reached over to open the passenger door for Zaniyah. She didn't say a word as she got in. Her eyes did all the talking. They bounced around in their sockets, searching for signs of danger.

Signs of Jah.

Zo took the Ruger pistol off his hip and set it down on his lap. Like Zaniyah, he, too, was leery of Jah. He looked around to make sure the street was clear before he started the engine and drove off.

"So," Zaniyah asked, pulling her hair back in a ponytail, "that was your mom, huh?"

Zo nodded his head yes.

"Wow. She looks bad."

"I know."

"You should get her some help."

"Only help she wants is help getting her next high. Ain't nothing I can do to help her. She's been like that since I was a baby. Just getting worse, that's all. Fucking around with that meth. Shit got her all fucked up."

"You need to be extremely careful with how you handle this beef with Jah. I'm telling you what's real. He's been dropping bodies since he was a kid. He won't hesitate when he sees you. I know grown-ass men who are literally terrified of that boy."

Zo shrugged. He, too, had been afraid of Jah, but now that his little brother was dead, he didn't care about dying. Whenever he crossed paths with Jah, it was going down on sight: simple as that. Whether or not he died trying to kill Jah no longer mattered to him. At this point, he was ready to open fire on Jah as soon as possible, even if it was in front of a police station. One way or another, Jah was going to pay for killing Roddy.

"You need to watch out for that nigga you was hanging with earlier, too. That nigga Kendrick. My cousin just texted me a few minutes ago saying somebody got ten bands on his head. They say he a snitch."

Zo thought back to the ride he'd taken with Lashaunda and Kendrick. He'd had a feeling that something was wrong about Kendrick coming home so soon. He was glad that he hadn't thrown Kendrick any drugs to get on with.

Just then, an older model Lincoln pulled up alongside his door as he stopped at a red light on 16th Street.

The Lincoln's passenger window rolled down. Zo chuckled once when he saw that it was Kendrick behind the wheel.

"What up, young nigga? I heard what happened to your lil bruh. Damn, that must've went down right after me and Shaunda dropped you back off, huh? See? We should've just pushed on 'em from the jump. We could've ran right up in the

155

crib. But don't trip. I got a plan. I got a way to get 'em and come up at the same time. All we gotta do is wait for a lil bit. Just don't go at 'em tonight. Let me work my magic. I promise you that by morning you won't have to worry about that nigga Jah ever again."

"I ain't worried about him now," Zo said, trying to sound cocky and confident in front of Zaniyah.

Kendrick gave an understanding nod of the head. "I already know. Just giving you a heads up. Lil niggas don't know who they fuckin' with. I'm about to show 'em what—"

It all happened within a second or two.

A dark colored Ford had just pulled up behind Kendrick's old-school Lincoln.

The traffic light had just turned green.

The driver and the passenger doors of the Ford flew open, and two youngsters with dreadlocks hanging over their faces got out of the car. One of them had an AK-47 and the other had a Tec-9.

They ran up from both sides of the Lincoln and opened fire on Kendrick.

Frightened and shocked by the sudden change of events, Zo slammed his foot down on the gas pedal. Zaniyah screamed and slid down in her seat. The Chevy's tires screeched as Zo rocketed forward up 16th Street.

Chapter 30

'Handled that lord. Just slide on me with the ten racks'

A glorious smile crossed Rell's face as he read the text message. He looked over at Tamera, who was propelling the big black Escalade down Madison Street.

After waiting at Northwestern Memorial Hospital while Tirzah was examined and questioned regarding the rape, they had picked up Maria and taken her and Dora back to the hotel before heading out for the concert. Momma had talked Jah out of $200 for babysitting, and Jah was still pouting about it.

The minor bruising on Tirzah's face was for the most part hidden behind a layer of makeup. She was looking beautiful sitting next to Jah, though her facial expression told the story of how hurt she felt inside. She and Tamera had both changed into tight-fitting 7 Jeans and sweatshirts over Giuseppe Zanotti heels. They both looked thick and fine enough to be in the next big rap video.

To Jah, Rell said, "One down, two to go. Just got a text from Johnny B. Kendrick's outta there."

Tamera's eyes widened. "Dead?" she murmured.

Rell nodded.

Jah said, "Good. Ol' police-ass nigga. Tamera, I hope you ain't got no more police-ass exes that's gon' be coming tryna extort a nigga. You see how the mob handle that shit."

Tamera rolled her eyes. Rell leaned over to her and kissed her on the cheek.

"Baby only got me. Ain't that right?" Rell said.

Tamera was too stunned by the news of Kendrick's murder to respond.

"Now," Jah said, "all we gotta do is catch up with Zo and that pussy nigga Tremaine. I really wanna get Tremaine myself. Nigga wanna rape my woman. I'ma let him rape the hole in this pistol."

"I just hope he's really dead. And I hope he didn't talk to that cop," Rell said just as another message caused his smartphone to vibrate.

It was a video.

He pressed play. Whoever recorded the video had done it from the backseat of a car that was parked behind an older model Lincoln Continental at a traffic light. Johnny B and Lil Larry were just getting out of the front seats.

Rell held the phone up so that Jah could also see it.

Tirzah gasped as the gunfire started.

"Haha. Bitch," Jah said.

Rell clenched his teeth together and dropped his chin to his chest, as if the bullets were flying at him. He almost felt bad for Kendrick. It was a shame that Kendrick had to go out in such a brutal way. If he'd been a man and handled his beef with Rell in a street way, he might have lived. Instead, he'd resorted to being a snitch, in the number-one city where snitching meant certain death.

Rell played the video twice more and then deleted the message. A deafening silence followed.

They were just passing Madison Street Barbers. The massive white dome of the United Center loomed a few blocks ahead. Traffic was congested with concertgoers who could not wait to get inside the stadium and get a glimpse of some of their hometown's greatest recording artists. Rell had a blunt of Kush burning and an ounce of it in his pocket for the backstage show.

It took Tamera ten minutes to find a parking spot. Rell loved seeing the huge diamond glistening on her finger. She seemed to get happier every time she looked at it.

Jah's connect came through for them. They went in through a different entrance than the other concertgoers. Big Rick introduced them to Liffy Stokes and Twista as they were entering a smoked-out dressing room.

Rell found a chair in the back of the room and took a seat. Tamera sat on his lap. He talked to Twista, Liffy, and Mayz and told them how much he loved their music. He listened to them talk about the current state of the music industry. They got up and took some pictures together before sitting back down to blow more blunts.

"We should've brought K and Tara with us," Tamera said. "I know they would have loved the opportunity to meet some of these rappers."

"K already done met Twista, at a video shoot for Sicko Mobb. Tara was there, too." Rell sucked in a mouthful of Kush smoke. "Plus, I'm pretty sure that they're enjoying their Valentine's Day in that hotel room. We need to hurry up and get back there ourselves. I got some new moves I looked up on Google. Gon' break your back with 'em, too."

Tamera rolled her eyes and laughed. It was a sweet, soft laugh. Rell realized that he loved absolutely everything about Tamera. He smiled thoughtfully at her while she swept her eyes around the room. To him, Tamera Lyon was a bigger star than all of the rappers combined.

He had a feeling that his father was smiling down from heaven, proud that his son had chosen wisely. Tamera was the woman of Rell's dreams, and he could not wait to give her the world.

Chapter 31

"And my mother and my grandmother cocoa butter kisses
This is just a testament to the ones that raised me, the ones
that I praise and I'm thanking I need 'em, but the chronic all
up in my clothes
And I wanna get a hug, and I can't 'cause I'm stanking
Never too old for a spanking..."

Twista was just finishing up his verse on Chance The
Rapper's "Cocoa Butter Kisses" when the music suddenly
stopped.

Tamera, Tirzah, Rell, and Jah were standing off to the
side of the stage, watching the performance. They all looked
at each other and then looked down at the thick black cords
near their feet, thinking that maybe they had accidentally un-
plugged one.

The crowd got quiet as they, too, wondered what had
malfunctioned.

Then Big Rick walked out to the stage with a microphone
in hand and spoke:

"Love is a beautiful thing, ain't it? Black love, white love
— whatever. It's just good. If you're married, give me a shout
right quick."

A bunch of people in the crowd shouted and threw their
hands in the air.

"That's what it's about right there. That's exactly what
it's about. You gotta find yourselves a good partner that'll
hold you up through all the downs. Me and my wife been together eight years now. I ain't saying it's been all fun, but I
know it would've been a whole lot harder had I done it alone.
With that being said, I'd like to introduce y'all to my boy Jah.
Come on out, Jah."

Jah was more nervous than he'd ever been as he grabbed Tirzah's hand and walked out to the stage with her, eyeing the huge crowd, glimpsing live video of himself and Tirzah on the massive overhead screens. Her eyes were just as wide as his, though he was in on the surprise.

Thinking back to the relationship he'd had with Felicia, he could never remember feeling the way he felt now. He loved Felicia, but not anywhere near as much as he loved Tirzah. He realized now that he had broken up with Tirzah this morning because he'd been afraid. He loved her so much that it scared him. She was perfect in every way — thick where it counted, pretty in the face, loyal, classy, and virtuous.

Big Rick handed Jah the mic.

He took the jewelry box out of his pocket and quickly got down on one knee while Tirzah was looking back at Tamera.

When she turned and saw that he was kneeled in front of her she slapped her hands over her mouth and immediately teared up.

"You know I love you more than I've ever loved any-body," Jah said into the mic, looking up at Tirzah as the audience cheered him on. "I'm one of the hardest niggas in the streets, but when I woke up this morning, I was scared. I was scared of loving you. I had to do some serious thinking, and I came to the conclusion that it's about that time for me to wake up and grow up. I gotta step up and be the man my pops wanted me to be."

He flipped open the lid on the jewelry box, and the crowd went wild. Out of the corner of his eye, he saw Rell and Tamera clapping their hands and beaming happily. The rap artists who had already performed were also clapping their hands as they came out to the stage.

Tirzah was crying as she stared down at Jah. She looked breathtakingly beautiful in her skintight jeans and heels. Her hair was on point, as was her makeup. Her fingernails were manicured and painted to perfection. Even the tears that were rolling down her perfect face looked amazing.

"Tirzah Lyon," Jah said, and took a deep breath. "Will you marry me?"

Chapter 32

Tirzah said yes.

She had never even contemplated what she would say if Jah ever proposed to her, but when he did, the answer came naturally, as if she had been preparing for that moment all her life.

Their kiss seemed to last forever. Her ears were still ringing from the sound of the crowd screaming as she and Jah had kissed.

Now they were stumbling into their hotel suite, kissing and rubbing all over each other. Tirzah wasn't sure what she would do once they made it to bed. She didn't want to have sex. Not after she'd been raped. The doctors and nurses at Northwestern Memorial had warned her to hold off on sexual relations, at least until the test results came back.

But with the way she was feeling right now, she wasn't sure if she could hold off. And besides, it wasn't like Tremaine could have done any vaginal damage. His dick was so small that she'd hardly even felt it. The only thing she was really concerned about was an STD. As long as he hadn't given her something that could not be healed, she was fine. She had been given a pill that would prevent a pregnancy from the rape.

Jah picked her up and threw her onto the bed. She was all smiles as she bounced up and down on the soft mattress. Jah took off his jacket and hoodie and tossed them to the floor. He started unbuckling his Hermes belt.

"I think we should wait," Tirzah said, wincing as if Jah was going to slap her with his belt buckle for turning him down. "Can we just lay together? Please?"

Surprisingly, Jah didn't argue with her. He got in bed next to her, and she mounted him and kissed him on the mouth. Their tongues mingled. She inhaled the delicious scent of his cologne and let out an involuntary moan as she felt his dick hardening between her thighs. She wanted so badly to take it out and impale herself on it. She knew how good it would feel inside her.

"How you gon' tell me I can't get none and then sit that pussy right on me?" Jah said as he rubbed on her ass. "What kinda sense does that make?"

"Oh, shut up." Tirzah sucked her teeth and smiled. She thought for a moment and then continued. "Listen. There are some ground rules you're gonna have to follow if you plan on having me as your wife."

"What kinda ground rules?"

"Well, for one, you can't be just going out and killing people when you're mad. That's not gonna cut it. I'm sorry. I can't deal with that kinda shit. I'm all with having a gangsta ass nigga for a hubby but not a fool. Be a gangsta when the time is right. Your first priority should be to take care of home and keep me happy. Happy wife, happy life. You got that?"

Jah nodded.

"Second," Tirzah sailed on, "you're gonna have to grow up real fast. I know you're still young, but that's no excuse. Especially here in Chicago. Young niggas out here go through more than the average man goes through his entire life. You're about to be eighteen. Are you sure I'm the one you can see yourself spending the rest of your life with? Because if not, you can have this ring back right fucking now, and I mean that. I know my worth, and I won't be shortchanged."

Jah nodded his head in agreement. "I'm with you all the way on that," he said. "As long as you remain faithful to me, I'm here for you. Really, the only thing I'd be worried about is you fucking another nigga."

"Boy, please." She rolled her eyes. "This pussy is yours. That's not even a question. I haven't even thought about stepping out on you. I have faith in you. I know that if your brother can love my lil sister like that, then I know you can love me the same way. You and Rell got the same parents. Y'all got the same heart." She poked the tip of an index fingernail into his chest. "We're going to go through some things. Ups and downs are normal, Jah. You have to understand that. Get that through your head. Please. Because I don't need you leaving me when shit gets tough. I need a man who will stick by my side through it all. Through every storm, not just through the sunny days."

Jah nodded again. "I'm with you, baby. That's on my dead niggas."

"You don't need to put it on anybody's grave. Just be a man of your word and hold me down."

"I got'chu."

"I hope so."

"You should know so," he said.

"You certainly didn't have me this morning. Asshole. Give me a kiss." She lowered her mouth to his, and this time when they finished kissing, she fixed her braids in a ponytail and moved back until her face was right over his unbuckled belt.

Slowly, she slid the belt off and then unzipped his jeans and tugged them down a bit, looking up to him and biting her bottom lip.

He smiled like a fat kid in a candy factory.

Tirzah laughed. "Look at you. Horny ass."

"Ain't nothing wrong with being horny. We got seven billion mu'fuckas on earth 'cause their parents got horny. God made us to be horny. That's why he gave me this big dick. It's why he gave you that big mouth."

"To bite it off?"

Jah's eyes got large. "Hey, now. We ain't on that shit," he said with a chuckle.

Tirzah wasn't on that shit either. She pulled out his heavy phallus and let it slap down onto his abdomen. She ran her tongue up its underside and then back down to his balls. She sucked his scrotum into her mouth and jerked his dick in her left hand, staring at the gleaming diamond engagement ring and hoping that the love she had with Jahlil Owens would last until her very last days.

Chapter 33

"I'm so excited for Jah and Tirzah. Your little hardheaded brother actually has a heart in that cold little chest of his."

"You can get off my lil nigga's chest," Rell said, laughing as he stepped into the Jacuzzi with Tamera, holding the neck of a bottle of Hennessy in one hand and an enormous four-gram blunt of Kush in the other.

He wore only a pair of boxer briefs and his necklace with the Jesus piece. Tamera had on a white two-piece bikini that had Rell practically drooling over her.

She lit the blunt for him while he popped open the cognac. They started drinking straight from the bottle. He noticed how intensely she stared at him as he canted his head back and blew a stream of smoke at the ceiling. He had to smile. Now that he and Jah were engaged to the beautiful Lyon sisters, he knew that his father's wishes had come to pass. Pops had always preached the importance of them marrying, and though Pops had not been a racist, he had been a firm believer in the power of Black love.

"You're thinking way too hard right now." Tamera adjusted her bikini top. "What's going on in that screwed up brain of yours? Thinking about calling off the engagement?"

"Ha!" Rell turned to his lady. "You serious? Never. I will never leave you. If anything you'll leave me."

"Mm hmm. That's what they all say until some pretty lil tenderoni comes walking by. Then all the vows go out the window and divorce comes blasting through the door."

"Divorce? You'd divorce me?"

"If you cheated on me, I most certainly would. I'm not sticking around for a single day. Hell, look at Charlie Sheen. Was messing around with all those girls and now his ass is stuck with HIV. I'm not interested in catching any kinds of diseases from you or anyone else. You'd be a fool to cheat on me, anyway. Am I not the business?"

Tamera stood up and did a full 360° turn. Rell reached out and squeezed on her ass. She was definitely a great catch. He'd never had a girlfriend so flawlessly fine and real. She drank from the fifth of Hennessy. Her expression twisted as the stinging liquor made its way down to her stomach.

"You are definitely the business," Rell said. He toked on the thickly stuffed blunt. "You ain't gotta worry, baby. I promise that I'll never even touch another woman unless it's a hug or a handshake. I told you, I like the taste of pussy too much to be cheating. I'm not about to be licking on no random thots."

"Yeah?" A conspiratorial smirk appeared on Tamera's face. She hooked a finger in the front of her bikini bottom and pulled it aside so that Rell could see her vaginal lips. "Hungry? Why wait?"

Rell laughed and gazed hungrily at her pussy. She fixed the bikini bottom and sat back down just as he was leaning forward to get a taste of his favorite meal.

"You gon' just tease a nigga like that?" he said.

She rolled her eyes, still smirking as she raised her left hand to look at the ring. The Jacuzzi was steaming hot and bubbling fiercely. She moved closer to Rell and took another swig from the bottle before handing it over to him.

Her pretty brown eyes remained on the diamond ring.

"It's crazy how this ring came about, isn't it?" she said. "It's almost like I was destined to have it. You brought it out to show it to me right when Big Man and Susan left for Miami. Then something happened and I ended up not taking it off. Susan had your dad calling every hour on the hour trying to get you to mail this ring to them. Every time you got ready to mail it off, something else happened. Then she died without ever getting the ring back, and now you've proposed to me with it." She shook her head. "Crazy."

"It is crazy. I can't explain that shit, either. Might have been destiny. You never know. I'm just glad that I was able to make you happy with it."

"*Happy* is an understatement. Bitches are going to be so jealous of me when they see this fat-ass diamond on my finger. I sent a picture of it to my mom. She went nuts on me. Said I better keep you because I'll never find another man who'll give me a ring like this and if you'd give me this, just imagine what else you'll give me."

"Big salute to your moms. Sounds like a smart woman to me."

"Oh, she is. And she's a bad bitch just like me and Tirz. Her ass is fatter than both of ours."

"Aw, you might wanna keep me away from her then. You fuck around and be my stepdaughter." Rell cracked up laughing and leaned away from Tamera as she took a swing at his head.

"Don't get fucked up, Jerrell."

"Why you only call me that when there's a threat behind it?"

"Because I want the real you to know that his nickname's about to get fucked up."

Rell chuckled and pecked his lips on the side of her neck. She moved over and got between his legs. Resting her back against his chest, she raised her hand yet again. This time they both studied the ring.

"We're getting married," she said, more to herself than anything. "Unbelievable."

"You better believe it." Rell brushed his lips across the nape of her neck. "I couldn't have chosen a more worthy bride."

"Ooooh, bitches are gonna hate me so much. I hate to say it, but they're looking at you like a cash cow. They think Big Man owned a lot more houses than he actually did. The girls at the salon were talking about it. I was mad at first, but then I said fuck it. It's not like they can get what's mine."

Tamera sighed and got quiet while Rell drank and smoked his blunt. He thought of the successful hit on Kendrick and reminded himself to stop by the bank to get the $10,000 for Johnny B first thing tomorrow morning. He had a bunch of heroin stashed away at the Trumbull Avenue house that he knew could take the place of the cash. He'd gotten it from Tamera. Just the thought of all she'd done for him since the day they met compelled him to plant yet another kiss on her neck.

"I'm telling you right now, Rell. I'm a little bit crazy. Don't say I didn't warn you."

"What kinda shit is that?"

"It's the truth. I don't think you realize it yet. I'm just letting you know now."

"Don't you think you should've told me that before I asked you to marry me?"

She shrugged her shoulders and changed the topic of conversation to wedding gowns. Rell listened without much interest. His mind was on Zo and what the young punk had done to Felicia. He had another $10,000 on Zo's head, but he knew that the hit on Zo would be more risky since Zo also had long money. It would take nothing for Zo to double the bounty and turn it on Rell and Jah. Rell trusted Johnny B, but not enough to put his life in Johnny B's hands. In the streets of Chicago/Chiraq, money talked and bullshit walked a thousand miles in the opposite direction. He'd known a great many mobsters and hustlers who'd fallen victim to betrayal from some of their closest friends, all because of the almighty dollar. He wasn't about to be the next example.

His ruminations came to an end when Tamera stood up a moment later and stepped out of the Jacuzzi. His eyes followed her every move. Her walk was hypnotic. Her curves were mouthwatering. She pinched the fabric of her bikini bottom out from between her jiggling cheeks as she walked to the bathroom.

Rell got out of the Jacuzzi and followed her, with the erection in his boxer briefs leading the way.

Chapter 34

The snow was coming down hard. There was a snow storm brewing outside, and Zo was watching it from Zaniyah's living room window.

The scent of well-seasoned ground beef drifted into the room from the kitchen. Zaniyah was cooking, and her friend Lisa was keeping her company in the kitchen while Zo stood alone in the living room, smoking a cigarette and reminiscing about all the good and bad times he'd shared with his little brother.

He and Roddy had gone through hell and back as kids in the North Lawndale neighborhood. He could not count the nights they'd spent sitting up and telling each other jokes they had learned at school, their stomachs growling harder than irritated pit bulls, their bodies reeking worse than the trash cans in the alley behind their sister's house. Although they had fought like cats and dogs (with Zo always coming out on top), Zo had loved Roddy more than anyone else in their family. No one understood Zo the way Roddy had. No one else had watched him cry because he had no money to get food for either of them. No one else knew about the night he'd lost his virginity to a crackhead in the alley on 15th and Trumbull. No one else had gone from rags to riches with him. Nobody but Roddy.

Zo kept wiping tears from his face as he stared out the blinds. He could see that Patricia was still sitting on Odella's front porch, no doubt waiting on him to return so that she could get him out of another $50. The policemen who had been posted on the block ever since Roddy's murder were now gone. The sky was pitch black. Cars were coming and going. Dope fiends were walking back and forth on Spaulding, wondering if he was going to open up business again tonight.

Sooner or later they would move on to another drug spot to cop some blow. Then they would see him later and complain that they had come to spend with him but ended up going somewhere else and getting some bullshit dope because he had closed down shop. He was used to it all by now.

He noticed that his hands were ashy. He told Zaniyah to bring him some lotion and seconds later she walked into the living room with a bottle of cocoa butter lotion.

"I'm almost finished cooking," she said. "Lisa's leaving after dinner. You can stay if you wanna. I don't have anybody coming over."

Zo nodded his head and turned to Zaniyah. He could not count on all his fingers and toes the number of times he'd masturbated to the vision of him fucking her senseless. He'd always thought that they were perfect for each other. Zo and Zaniyah. Just the sound of their names in the same sentence had brought an overwhelming joy to him. Roddy used to make fun of him for his crush on her. The guys at school had sometimes joked that the reason he never had lunch money was because he always tricked it off on Zaniyah. Now that he had her ready to do what he'd wanted to do for the past four or five years, he found that he didn't want it as bad as he thought he would.

"I'm so sorry about Roddy," she said, gently scraping her fingernails across his jaw. She moved in close and hugged him. "Jah will get what's coming to him. You better believe it. Karma's a bitch. She'll get his ass a hundred times worse. There's no way he's gonna just be able to keep killing people like that. Either he's gonna get snitched on, or he's gonna get killed. I guarantee it."

"I'ma whack that nigga myself." Zo's hurt voice was hardly above a whisper. He put his hands on Zaniyah's hips. "What we gon' do tonight? I need some kinda excitement."

"I've got all the excitement you need. You wait and see," Zaniyah said.

She headed back to the kitchen, and Zo took a seat on the sofa. He chain smoked Newport cigarettes and gazed vacantly at the television until Zaniyah brought him a plate, all the while conspiring to end the issue he had with Jah once and for all.

Chapter 35

The Hennessy she'd ingested had Tamera Lyon's head spinning. It also had her pussy throbbing.

She was patting her skin dry with a bath towel and looking at herself in the bathroom mirror when Rell walked up behind her and ripped off her bikini bottom. She felt the head of his hard pole slide in between her ass cheeks, but she didn't look back. She felt his lips on her shoulder as she wiped the droplets of water off the front of her neck.

When she finally looked at him in the mirror, she saw the hunger in his sexy eyes. He had his boxer briefs down to his knees. The blunt he'd been smoking was nowhere to be seen, and the bottle of Hennessy in his hand was halfway empty.

She inhaled sharply as she felt his huge erection slide into her pussy. He put a hand on her hip and slid in deeper. She planted her hands on the sink and arched her back as he began to thrust.

The reflection in the mirror of him fucking her from behind was sexier than any porn she'd ever watched. He had muscles like a WWE wrestler, and a bunch of gangster-looking tattoos that she could tell had been done during his time in prison. He set down the Hennessy bottle on the sink and leaned back a little as he slid in and out, in and out, penetrating her deeper with every thrust. His enormous love stick gave her a mixture of pain and pleasure, and again she found herself looking down at the ring. If this was what she had to look forward to for the rest of her life, she was all in.

Ten more minutes passed before they changed positions.

She sat on the sink and scooted to the edge, rapidly massaging her clitoris as he reentered her and sank all the way in. Her breath caught in her throat, and she didn't exhale until he was sliding out of her. She loved the way his abdominal muscles flexed as he put in his work.

"This my pussy right here," he said through clenched teeth. "Ain't it mine? Ain't it mine, baby?"

"Yes. Yes. Yes," Tamera replied in between gasps.

She eyed his dick as it drilled her harder and harder. Her juices coated its length. His balls were large and black and swinging merrily with every stroke. The wet sounds coming from her pussy made her moan louder as she realized just how deeply he was fucking her.

It was times like this when she was grateful that she was still young and in great physical shape. Her waist was perfectly slender and her abs were almost as tight as Rell's. She looked good sitting the way she was on the cool marble sink.

He put one of her legs on his shoulder and pounded her snug juice box with his wrist-thick phallus. Her vaginal muscles contracted as she experienced her first orgasm of the night, but Rell did not let up or slow down. Instead, he sped up. Tamera's moans became screams of delight. She clamped her hands onto the sink and held on for dear life as her fiancé hammered her pussy with deep, rough strokes.

Just then, there was a knock at the door of their hotel suite.

"Big cousin? Y'all busy in there?"

It was Tara.

Neither Rell nor Tamera responded.

Rell went even faster.

Tamera suspected that he was on the edge himself and she was right. He snatched his dick out of her just seconds later and sent a dozen long ribbons of cum flying across her abdomen, neck, and face. Some even got on the mirror. She had never seen so much semen come out of him. There was so much of it that she immediately smelled its salty odor.

He chuckled and took one step back. Slapping the head of his deflating love muscle on her clitoris, he said, "Damn. We gotta do this more often. That Henny hit the spot."

"No, nigga," Tamera said as she picked up the bottle of Hennessy and took a large gulp of the fiery liquor, "you hit the spot. The Henny only helped."

Chapter 36

Rell and Tamera put on their underwear and got in bed. Tamera turned on the television and went to abc7 News while Rell plugged the charger into his smartphone.

"Look." Tamera pointed at the TV.

There had been a homicide on 16th Street. It was Kendrick. Rell could tell that it was the same Lincoln from the video message Johnny B had sent him.

"That's his momma's car," Tamera said, shaking her head. "Wow. I'm shocked. I mean, not really, but damn, you know what I mean? I used to date that man. I never thought he'd turn into such a coward. I would have respected him more if he'd tried to rob us or something. But no, he wanted to be a snitch."

"That's what snitches get. You know that. I don't feel bad for the nigga. He shouldn't have been on that. Should've kept it a hundred."

"He's dead, Rell. Jesus."

"And my bro is free. Hurray."

Tamera laughed and slapped Rell on the knee. "You know what I'm saying. I'm tired of all the drama, baby. All the beefs. All the shootings. It really needs to stop."

"What about Tremaine?"

"Oh, hell no. He raped my sister. He should have been right there next to Kendrick."

"He'll get it the same way. Believe that. Ain't no way Jah gon' let that slide."

"Jah doesn't have to do a thing. I'll do it myself. The next time I see that motherfucker, he's dead. And I mean that."

Rell believed her. She had killed before. Twice, in fact. At the same time. He knew that she would not hesitate to blow Tremaine's brains out when the time came.

There was another knock at the door.

"Yes?" Tamera said as she pushed the covers down.

"It's me again," Tara said. "Sorry to be bugging y'all. Won't be but a minute. Need a word with my cousin and I'll be out of your way."

Tamera looked at Rell and he gave her a nod. She got up and went to the door and returned with Tara. Rell smiled at his dear cousin. She was reddish-brown-skinned like Tirzah, and she wore glasses.

Tara crossed her arms over her chest and regarded Rell and Tamera with a small grin as Tamera climbed back into bed.

"What?" Rell said, still beaming.

Tara shook her head and said nothing.

"The hell are you looking at me like that for?" Rell said.

"It's just amazing, that's all. I'm a little surprised. Never thought I'd see you settle down and be happy with one woman, and I definitely didn't expect Jah to do it. Good to see he's following in your footsteps. You're a good role model."

"Is that all?"

Tara shook her head no. "I know it's late, and I really don't want to tell you this knowing how it's gonna end up getting handled, but I have some info for you. An address. One that I'm sure you'll love having."

Rell stared at her and waited.

"A friend of mine knows where Tremaine has been laying his head. It's a house on Kildare in K-Town, right off Chicago Avenue. My girl Shanita — y'all know Shanita, the one who lives two houses down from auntie Maria — but anyway, her brother does business with Tremaine. I would have told Jah, but I don't want him going out at this time of night. You know he'll rush right over there. Plus, y'all have to be prepared for what you're gonna have to deal with once you get over there. It's not going to be a cakewalk."

Rell's smile turned upside down. So did Tamera's. They gazed at Tara with calculating eyes.

"Tremaine's a high-ranking Unknown Vice Lord," Tara went on. "He has a few hundred gangbangers working beneath him. Some real savages. From what I hear, they're almost always around him, especially when he feels threatened. I'm pretty sure he knows you and Jah are gonna be at his head over what he did to Tirzah. Don't go rushing out there to get him. Think it over. Sleep on it. And whatever you do, don't let Jah know anything about it tonight. Let him rest. I'll give you the exact address first thing in the morning."

Rell tried staying awake after Tara left to think about what she had just told him, but he and Tamera were knocked out within minutes.

Chapter 37

When Zo woke up, Zaniyah was asleep next to him. She had apparently gotten up sometime during the night and put on a sweatshirt. It was cold, and either her heat was broken or it was malfunctioning.

Zo quickly put on his clothes and jacket and left the bedroom without waking Zaniyah. He checked his gun to make sure it wasn't on safety before he stepped outside.

He crossed the street to his sister's house and found that everyone was still in bed. He took a shower and put on a new outfit, then made himself a big bowl of cereal and ate it before he headed back out.

He got in his Cadillac and drove to the convenience store on 16th and Drake to get a pack of cigarettes and a few packages of Backwoods cigarillos. He ended up adding a bunch of snacks to the counter before making his purchase.

Azid, the Arab guy behind the register, gave him a head nod as he rang up the items. He knew Azid from seeing him in the store every day, and once they'd bumped into each other at a movie theater.

"They find the guy who did that to your brother yet?" Azid asked. Then he added, "Not trying to be all up in your nose. If you don't want to talk because of grief I understand."

"All up in my nose?" Zo laughed for the first time since learning of his brother's murder. "You need to take some more English classes, my nigga. That shit ain't gon' work. And nah, they ain't get the nigga yet. He's good as got, though. As soon as he comes back to the hood his life is over."

"In my country, in Lebanon, we give street justice when people hurt kids. And police help. One time a man killed his wife and daughter and we beat him to death and tied him to the back of a motorcycle and dragged him. Drag him through the town. Let all see it to know how not to be. Jail is not for everything. Some need death for their acts. Their actions. Some must die. It's better because they are just scum, you know what I mean?"

Zo nodded. He definitely understood what Azid meant. He handed Azid a twenty-dollar bill.

"There was a guy in here yesterday who I remember vividly," Azid continued. "Kendrick is his name. He was always nice to me. Nice to my wife. He got killed because they say he worked with police. Yesterday. Is that true?"

Zo gave Azid another nod.

"Then he deserve it, too, you know. If you're out here doing the bad stuff yourself, then you should die for working with police because you're no man. No real man would do that. Stick to the rules. That's my opinion."

"I'm with you all the way, Azid. These rat-ass niggas out here snitchin' like it's in style but claiming they with the shits. This shit don't work like that. You either in or you out. Ain't no fuckin' in between."

It was Azid's turn to nod his head in agreement. He handed Zo the change he had left from the $20 and a plastic bag.

"You be safe out here," Azid said as Zo pushed open the door.

He bumped right into Johnny B as he was walking out.

They both froze and stared at each other. Zo knew that Johnny B was one of Jah's guys off 13th and Avers, and he was pretty sure that Johnny B knew all about the beef he had with Jah.

"My bad. Didn't see you," Johnny B said.

Zo said nothing at first. Then, just as Johnny B was about to turn and walk in the store, Zo said, "He got money on my head, too, don't he?"

188

"I don't know what you're talkin' about," Johnny B said.

"You know what I'm talkin' about. Jah. I was right there at the red light when Kendrick got offed. Just wanna know if I should be expecting the same shit. If he got money on my head, I got triple whatever he's offering on his. And that's on my lil brotha."

There was a glint of something in Johnny B's eyes, something that was not hidden by the long dreadlocks that concealed most of his face.

Was it betrayal? Was he ready to go against Jah for the right sum of money?

Whatever it was encouraged Zo to keep pushing. He gave Johnny B the name he could search for to find his Facebook page and told him to contact him there if he wanted the money, and he wasn't surprised when Johnny B saved the information in a smartphone before heading into the store.

Chapter 38

There were ten young gang members standing outside on the corner of Kildare and Chicago Avenue when Rell and Jah rode by in a brand-new black Mercedes Benz S550.

They looked around for Tremaine's green Jaguar, and Rell kept driving when they didn't see it.

The Benz was a rental. Rell had gotten it right after they checked out of the hotel this morning. It was so nice inside that now he was considering purchasing one.

"I can rock with this," he said to Jah as he drove down Chicago Avenue. "This my first time driving a Benz. Now I see why niggas love 'em so much. Look how smooth it rides."

"Bruh, I could give two fucks how smooth this mu'fucka rides. I just wanna catch this nigga who hurt my baby. And don't forget we gotta drop that bread off to Johnny B. You know his thirsty ass waiting on that shit."

"Fuck it, we can ride over there and do that now." Rell had already stopped by the bank and withdrew the $10,000 he owed Johnny B. It was in his pocket with his own bundle of hundreds. "We'll just keep sliding through here looking for that Jag throughout the day. Buy a few sacks of loud to throw 'em off. Soon's we see his ass, we can just air him out and smash off before his lil guys can shoot back. Piece of cake."

"I wouldn't give a fuck if they did shoot back," Jah said, picking up the Mac-10 submachine gun from the floor between his Jordan sneakers. It had a 50-shot clip sticking out from under it, and there was another 50-shot clip that went to it in Jah's hoodie pocket. "This mu'fucka fully auto. Let a nigga try to shoot it out with me if they want to. I dare 'em to. I can't wait to let this bitch shake some shit. On Neal, I'ma knock a nigga clean out his socks with this hoe. That nigga

Tremaine ain't gon' be raping nobody else. I can bet money on that."

"Call Johnny B and tell him to meet us at the crib on Trumbull," Rell said. "Nah, better yet, tell him to meet us at Momma's house. Trumbull probably ain't the best place to be after that fuck nigga shot Felicia yesterday. Tell Johnny B we got his money right now, and I took out the extra ten bands just in case they hit up that nigga Zo, too."

"I wanna get Zo myself, bruh." Jah dialed a number on his smartphone. "We ain't gotta pay nobody to hit him up. I know where his sister stay. I should slide through and light her whole house up, since punk-ass niggas wanna shoot through doors and shit."

Rell laughed and turned on some music while Jah talked to Johnny B. He looked around at the interior of the Mercedes. There was plush white leather and woodgrain everywhere. The seats were heated and as comfortable as his bed, and it had that proverbial "new car" smell.

Both he and Jah wore black hoodies and sweatpants with black-and-red Jordan sneakers. Their Jesus pieces gleamed on their chests. Rell had his Glock laying on his lap, and as bad as he wanted to fly away with his beautiful bride-to-be, he knew that the beefs with Tremaine and Zo had to be handled first. There was no way around it.

When Jah got off the line with Johnny B he said, "He want us to meet him on D Block. He say they over there smokin' and drinkin' anyway. It's D-Lo Day. I had forgot his Soulday was today."

D-Lo was a childhood friend of Jah's who'd been shot and killed this past December. The street they were born and raised on — 13th and Avers — was now called "D Block" in D-Lo's honor.

"Let's stop by the L and get some bottles for the gang," Jah suggested. "You know D-Lo used to drink that Remy all day. We gotta grab some of that."

Rell was in agreement. He would buy at least ten bottles of Remy Martin to drink with the guys and girls on his block. He knew how proud they would be of him when they saw him pull up in the sleek black Benz. No one from their block had ever driven a foreign car. He would be the first.

He realized that he was thinking the same way he'd told Jah not to think, but he couldn't help it. The Benz had him feeling invincible. He had lived the majority of his life either in poverty or very close to it. Now that he had over a million dollars in the bank and a Benz at his fingertips, he felt that it was only right to splurge a little.

"Hope we can catch that nigga Tremaine, big bruh," Jah said as he set the Mac-10 back on the floor. "If we can get him and Zo out the way, on Daddy I'm done with this street shit. I'ma take your advice and just get married and be happy. Fuck it."

Rell chuckled and put a hand on Jah's head. "You learned from the best, young man. Now let's get over to Johnny B and give him this money before he tries to shoot us next."

King Rio

194

Chapter 39

Using the money Johnny B gave her to cook for D-Lo's birthday celebration, Shanita Lewis bought and cooked a bunch of hot wings, cheesy spaghetti, green beans, corn on the cob, mac and cheese, and fudge brownies. She was thirty-seven years old, and she knew that Johnny B was just eighteen, but she had a crush on the young thug and she thought that accepting the cooking offer might open up other opportunities. She was a cougar at heart, always flirting with the younger guys whenever she was around them, and giving a select few a bit of what she liked to refer to as her "Kit Kat".

She liked Johnny B. A lot. She was more than willing to break him off a piece of her Kit Kat whenever he wanted it.

She liked that he was tall and dark and handsome. She liked that he had all the girls in the neighborhood going wild over him. She liked that he had a savage reputation in the streets, so savage that he was often compared to Jah, the most hardened killer in the D Block clique of Vice Lords.

Shanita had the kind of body that kept the young guys shouting and staring. She had an enormous ass and a small waist and that was all the youngsters wanted to see, which is why she often left the house wearing snug-fitting jeans and leggings, or sweatpants with nothing underneath.

Today she had gone with the jeans.

She was walking through the house, making sure Johnny B's bad-ass friends and their girls weren't stealing or destroying her things, when she found Johnny B standing in her bathroom doorway with a plate full of hot wings.

He smiled at Shanita with greasy lips. "These mu'fuckas is fire," he said, sucking the sauce off his thumb. "I got another $50 for you soon's my nigga Rell get over here. Thanks for doing all this on such short notice. I appreciate it."

Shanita put her fists on her hips and looked up at Johnny B. "Anything for Johnny. Boy, how long you been growing those dreads?"

"Like six years. Why? My shit drapin', ain't it."

"Don't get a big head about it. They're cool, but they ain't all that."

"Don't lie to yourself like that." Johnny B's smile could light up a room.

Shanita rolled her eyes. "So," she asked, "Rell's been breaking bread with y'all, huh? I hear him and Jah got rich from the houses Big Man left 'em. That's crazy, too. I remember Big Man was a straight up dope head. He made a helluva change before he passed away. Left something to his kids. That's what it's all about."

Johnny B leaned to the side to cast a blatant glance at Shanita's backside. She giggled shyly.

"Boy, you better stop. Young ass."

"Rell ain't breakin' bread like he's supposed to be. He ain't gave us a whole lot. Jah threw me a few zips of boy. That's about it so far. I had to put in work for what's coming to me today."

"Life is all about hard work, Johnny. Like the work I'd put in on your young ass." Shanita grabbed the bottom of his shirt and held it in her fist as she looked up at him.

Then she turned and led him up the hallway, past two framed portraits of Jesus Christ and a wooden cross with Jesus on it that hung on the walls, and finally to her bedroom.

He put down his plate on her dresser and used a napkin to clean his fingers and wipe the grease off his lips. Shanita stood in front of him and put her hands on her hips as Johnny sat down on her bed.

"I got a question," he said, picking at his teeth with his pinkie fingernail.

"What kinda question?" Shanita asked.

"Let's just say your guy had a bunch of money and wanted to pay you to do something to an enemy, but the enemy had triple that amount for you to do the same thing to your guy. I'm talking thirty bands. What would you do?"

"Thirty bands? You mean thirty thousand dollars?"

Johnny B nodded his head yes.

"That's a lot of money, Johnny. Especially in this economy. It's fucked up around here. Most people can't even find a job, let alone thirty thousand dollars."

"That's what I'm saying to myself." Johnny B's expression became thoughtful. He wiped the food he'd picked from his teeth on the napkin and tossed it in the trashcan next to Shanita's bed. "I really don't wanna think that way. I really wanna just rock with my lil nigga. But it's a cold game, you feel me? Niggas out here starving. My family ain't got no money. Right about now I'm ready to do whatever to make sure my family eating. Even if that means going against the grain. I mean, this nigga's brother just proposed to his girl with a ring that look like it cost about a million dollars. If you ever saw that ring Big Man's wife had, then you know what I'm talking about. It's all on Facebook. Rell just proposed to Tamera with that big-ass diamond ring."

Shanita leaned back on her dresser and gazed at Johnny B for a long moment. She could tell that he was doing some serious thinking. She understood the meaning behind the scenario he'd just painted for her.

"Here's what I think you should do," she said. "I think you should just hold out for the perfect opportunity if you're gonna go against the grain. You can't fuck up under any circumstances. Don't rush into it. Just let it happen. I assume you're talking about Rell and Jah, right?"

Johnny nodded again.

"Just wait it out," Shanita repeated. "And if you end up coming up on something nice, just let me get the ring."

The two of them laughed.

A few minutes later, Rell pulled up out front in a black Mercedes Benz. Shanita watched from behind the screen door as Rell handed Johnny B a stack of cash before pulling over to park.

All Shanita could think about was the ring.

To Be Continued...
Mobbed Up 4
Coming Soon

Submission Guideline

Submit the first three chapters of your completed manuscript to ldpsubmissions@gmail.com, subject line: Your book's title. The manuscript must be in a .doc file and sent as an attachment. Document should be in Times New Roman, double spaced and in size 12 font. Also, provide your synopsis and full contact information. If sending multiple submissions, they must each be in a separate email.

Have a story but no way to send it electronically? You can still submit to LDP/Ca$h Presents. Send in the first three chapters, written or typed, of your completed manuscript to:

LDP: Submissions Dept
Po Box 944
Stockbridge, Ga 30281

DO NOT send original manuscript. Must be a duplicate.

Provide your synopsis and a cover letter containing your full contact information.

Thanks for considering LDP and Ca$h Presents.

<u>NEW RELEASES</u>

FRIEND OR FOE 3 by MIMI
A GANGSTA'S KARMA by FLAME
NIGHTMARE ON SILENT AVE by CHRIS
GREEN
THE STREETS MADE ME 3 by LARRY D.
WRIGHT
MOBBED UP 3 by KING RIO

GORILLAZ IN THE BAY V

3X KRAZY III

De'Kari

KINGPIN KILLAZ IV

STREET KINGS III

PAID IN BLOOD III

CARTEL KILLAZ IV

DOPE GODS III

Hood Rich

SINS OF A HUSTLA II

ASAD

RICH $AVAGE II

By Troublesome

YAYO V

Bred In The Game 2

S. Allen

CREAM III

By Yolanda Moore

SON OF A DOPE FIEND III

HEAVEN GOT A GHETTO II

By Renta

LOYALTY AIN'T PROMISED III

By Keith Williams

I'M NOTHING WITHOUT HIS LOVE II

SINS OF A THUG II

TO THE THUG I LOVED BEFORE II

By Monet Dragun

QUIET MONEY IV

EXTENDED CLIP III

THUG LIFE IV

By **Trai'Quan**

THE STREETS MADE ME IV

By **Larry D. Wright**

IF YOU CROSS ME ONCE II

By **Anthony Fields**

THE STREETS WILL NEVER CLOSE II

By **K'ajji**

HARD AND RUTHLESS III

Von Diesel

KILLA KOUNTY II

By **Khufu**

MOBBED UP IV

By **King Rio**

MONEY GAME II

By **Smoove Dolla**

A GANGSTA'S KARMA II

By **FLAME**

Available Now

RESTRAINING ORDER **I & II**

By **CA$H & Coffee**

LOVE KNOWS NO BOUNDARIES **I II & III**

By **Coffee**

King Rio

RAISED AS A GOON I, II, III & IV

BRED BY THE SLUMS I, II, III

BLAST FOR ME I & II

ROTTEN TO THE CORE I II III

A BRONX TALE I, II, III

DUFFLE BAG CARTEL I II III IV V VI

HEARTLESS GOON I II III IV V

A SAVAGE DOPEBOY I II

DRUG LORDS I II III

CUTTHROAT MAFIA I II

KING OF THE TRENCHES

By **Ghost**

LAY IT DOWN **I & II**

LAST OF A DYING BREED I II

BLOOD STAINS OF A SHOTTA I & II III

By **Jamaica**

LOYAL TO THE GAME I II III

LIFE OF SIN I, II III

By **TJ & Jelissa**

BLOODY COMMAS I & II

SKI MASK CARTEL I II & III

KING OF NEW YORK I II,III IV V

RISE TO POWER I II III

COKE KINGS I II III IV

BORN HEARTLESS I II III IV

KING OF THE TRAP I II

By **T.J. Edwards**

IF LOVING HIM IS WRONG…I & II

LOVE ME EVEN WHEN IT HURTS I II III

By **Jelissa**

WHEN THE STREETS CLAP BACK I & II III

THE HEART OF A SAVAGE I II III

By **Jibril Williams**

A DISTINGUISHED THUG STOLE MY HEART I II & III

LOVE SHOULDN'T HURT I II III IV

RENEGADE BOYS I II III IV

PAID IN KARMA I II III

SAVAGE STORMS I II

AN UNFORESEEN LOVE

By **Meesha**

A GANGSTER'S CODE I &, II III

A GANGSTER'S SYN I II III

THE SAVAGE LIFE I II III

CHAINED TO THE STREETS I II III

BLOOD ON THE MONEY I II III

By J-Blunt

PUSH IT TO THE LIMIT

By **Bre' Hayes**

BLOOD OF A BOSS **I, II, III, IV, V**

SHADOWS OF THE GAME

TRAP BASTARD

By **Askari**

THE STREETS BLEED MURDER **I, II & III**

THE HEART OF A GANGSTA I II& III

By **Jerry Jackson**

CUM FOR ME I II III IV V VI VII

An **LDP Erotica Collaboration**

BRIDE OF A HUSTLA **I II & II**

THE FETTI GIRLS **I, II& III**

CORRUPTED BY A GANGSTA I, II III, IV

BLINDED BY HIS LOVE

THE PRICE YOU PAY FOR LOVE I, II ,III

DOPE GIRL MAGIC I II III

By **Destiny Skai**

WHEN A GOOD GIRL GOES BAD

By **Adrienne**

THE COST OF LOYALTY I II III

By Kweli

A GANGSTER'S REVENGE **I II III & IV**

THE BOSS MAN'S DAUGHTERS I II III IV V

A SAVAGE LOVE **I & II**

BAE BELONGS TO ME I II

A HUSTLER'S DECEIT I, II, III

WHAT BAD BITCHES DO I, II, III

SOUL OF A MONSTER I II III

KILL ZONE

A DOPE BOY'S QUEEN I II

By **Aryanna**

A KINGPIN'S AMBITON

A KINGPIN'S AMBITION **II**

I MURDER FOR THE DOUGH

By **Ambitious**

TRUE SAVAGE I II III IV V VI VII

DOPE BOY MAGIC I, II, III

MIDNIGHT CARTEL I II III

CITY OF KINGZ I II

NIGHTMARE ON SILENT AVE

By **Chris Green**

A DOPEBOY'S PRAYER

By **Eddie "Wolf" Lee**

THE KING CARTEL **I, II & III**

By **Frank Gresham**

THESE NIGGAS AIN'T LOYAL **I, II & III**

By **Nikki Tee**

GANGSTA SHYT **I II &III**

By **CATO**

THE ULTIMATE BETRAYAL

By **Phoenix**

BOSS'N UP **I , II & III**

By **Royal Nicole**

I LOVE YOU TO DEATH

By **Destiny J**

I RIDE FOR MY HITTA

I STILL RIDE FOR MY HITTA

By **Misty Holt**

LOVE & CHASIN' PAPER

By **Qay Crockett**

TO DIE IN VAIN

SINS OF A HUSTLA
By **ASAD**
BROOKLYN HUSTLAZ
By **Boogsy Morina**
BROOKLYN ON LOCK I & II
By **Sonovia**
GANGSTA CITY
By **Teddy Duke**
A DRUG KING AND HIS DIAMOND I & II III
A DOPEMAN'S RICHES
HER MAN, MINE'S TOO I, II
CASH MONEY HO'S
THE WIFEY I USED TO BE I II
By Nicole Goosby
TRAPHOUSE KING **I II & III**
KINGPIN KILLAZ I II III
STREET KINGS I II
PAID IN BLOOD **I II**
CARTEL KILLAZ I II III
DOPE GODS I II
By **Hood Rich**
LIPSTICK KILLAH **I, II, III**
CRIME OF PASSION I II & III
FRIEND OR FOE I II III
By **Mimi**
STEADY MOBBN' **I, II, III**
THE STREETS STAINED MY SOUL I II

By **Marcellus Allen**

WHO SHOT YA **I, II, III**

SON OF A DOPE FIEND I II

HEAVEN GOT A GHETTO

Renta

GORILLAZ IN THE BAY **I II III IV**

TEARS OF A GANGSTA I II

3X KRAZY I II

DE'KARI

TRIGGADALE I II III

Elijah R. Freeman

GOD BLESS THE TRAPPERS I, II, III

THESE SCANDALOUS STREETS I, II, III

FEAR MY GANGSTA I, II, III IV, V

THESE STREETS DON'T LOVE NOBODY I, II

BURY ME A G I, II, III, IV, V

A GANGSTA'S EMPIRE I, II, III, IV

THE DOPEMAN'S BODYGAURD I II

THE REALEST KILLAZ I II III

THE LAST OF THE OGS I II III

Tranay Adams

THE STREETS ARE CALLING

Duquie Wilson

MARRIED TO A BOSS I II III

By Destiny Skai & Chris Green

KINGZ OF THE GAME I II III IV V

Playa Ray

SLAUGHTER GANG I II III
RUTHLESS HEART I II III
By Willie Slaughter
FUK SHYT
By Blakk Diamond
DON'T F#CK WITH MY HEART I II
By Linnea
ADDICTED TO THE DRAMA I II III
IN THE ARM OF HIS BOSS II
By Jamila
YAYO I II III IV
A SHOOTER'S AMBITION I II
BRED IN THE GAME
By S. Allen
TRAP GOD I II III
RICH $AVAGE
By Troublesome
FOREVER GANGSTA
GLOCKS ON SATIN SHEETS I II
By Adrian Dulan
TOE TAGZ I II III
LEVELS TO THIS SHYT I II
By Ah'Million
KINGPIN DREAMS I II III
By Paper Boi Rari
CONFESSIONS OF A GANGSTA I II III
By Nicholas Lock

I'M NOTHING WITHOUT HIS LOVE

SINS OF A THUG

TO THE THUG I LOVED BEFORE

By Monet Dragun

CAUGHT UP IN THE LIFE I II III

By Robert Baptiste

NEW TO THE GAME I II III

MONEY, MURDER & MEMORIES I II III

By **Malik D. Rice**

LIFE OF A SAVAGE I II III

A GANGSTA'S QUR'AN I II III

MURDA SEASON I II III

GANGLAND CARTEL I II III

CHI'RAQ GANGSTAS I II III

KILLERS ON ELM STREET I II III

JACK BOYZ N DA BRONX I II III

A DOPEBOY'S DREAM

By **Romell Tukes**

LOYALTY AIN'T PROMISED I II

By Keith Williams

QUIET MONEY I II III

THUG LIFE I II III

EXTENDED CLIP I II

By **Trai'Quan**

THE STREETS MADE ME I II III

By **Larry D. Wright**

THE ULTIMATE SACRIFICE I, II, III, IV, V, VI

KHADIFI

IF YOU CROSS ME ONCE

ANGEL I II

IN THE BLINK OF AN EYE

By **Anthony Fields**

THE LIFE OF A HOOD STAR

By **Ca$h & Rashia Wilson**

THE STREETS WILL NEVER CLOSE

By **K'ajji**

CREAM I II

By **Yolanda Moore**

NIGHTMARES OF A HUSTLA I II III

By **King Dream**

CONCRETE KILLA I II

By **Kingpen**

HARD AND RUTHLESS I II

MOB TOWN 251

By **Von Diesel**

GHOST MOB

Stilloan Robinson

MOB TIES I II

By **SayNoMore**

BODYMORE MURDERLAND I II III

By **Delmont Player**

FOR THE LOVE OF A BOSS

By **C. D. Blue**

MOBBED UP I II III
By King Rio
KILLA KOUNTY
By Khufu
MONEY GAME
By Smoove Dolla
A GANGSTA'S KARMA
By FLAME

BOOKS BY LDP'S CEO, CA$H

TRUST IN NO MAN

TRUST IN NO MAN 2

TRUST IN NO MAN 3

BONDED BY BLOOD

SHORTY GOT A THUG

THUGS CRY

THUGS CRY 2

THUGS CRY 3

TRUST NO BITCH

TRUST NO BITCH 2

TRUST NO BITCH 3

TIL MY CASKET DROPS

RESTRAINING ORDER

RESTRAINING ORDER 2

IN LOVE WITH A CONVICT

LIFE OF A HOOD STAR

Mobbed Up 3

CPSIA information can be obtained
at www.ICGtesting.com
Printed in the USA
LVHW082354150122
708614LV00013B/387

9 781955 270465